DARK REUNION

DARK REUNION

ALISON BROWNSTONE™ BOOK THIRTEEN

JUDITH BERENS MARTHA CARR MICHAEL ANDERLE

DISRUPTIVE IMAGINATION

LMBPN Publishing
PMB 196, 2540 South Maryland Pkwy
Las Vegas, NV 89109

First US edition, September 2019
eBook ISBN: 978-1-64202-484-5
Print ISBN: 978-1-64202-485-2

THE DARK REUNION TEAM

Thanks to the JIT Readers

Dave Hicks
Diane L. Smith
Dorothy Lloyd
Peter Manis
Jeff Eaton
John Ashmore
Jeff Goode
Paul Westman

If we've missed anyone, please let us know!

Editor
SkyHunter Editing Team

DEDICATIONS

From Martha

To everyone who still believes in magic
and all the possibilities that holds.
To all the readers who make this
entire ride so much fun.
And to my son, Louie and so many wonderful friends who
remind me all the time of what
really matters and how wonderful
life can be in any given moment.

From Michael

To Family, Friends and
Those Who Love
To Read.
May We All Enjoy Grace
To Live The Life We Are
Called.

CHAPTER ONE

D efenseless, tiny, and adorable. Those weren't words anyone would normally associate with a Brownstone but no one could deny they weren't appropriate for the baby in front of her.

Alison smiled at her infant brother, Thomas James Brownstone, who slumbered in the bassinet in her parent's living room. He lay on his back, his eyes closed and his tiny drool-covered thumb now beside his head. With his normal-looking skin and dark hair, he arguably resembled his mother more than his father, but given what Whispy Doom had told her father, her brother would inherit more than a few interesting traits from both parents.

No matter what, my little brother will definitely have an interesting future.

The littlest Brownstone had already created difficulty by being born early, which resulted in his father almost missing the whole event. James managed to make it in time and take care of a little unpleasantness associated with criminals shortly after. The Brownstone luck apparently applied even to the newly born but now, weeks later, Thomas caused no more trouble than a normal baby, at least as far as she could tell.

I really need to do something about portaling. This whole thing wouldn't have been a mess if I had been able to pull that off. Myna seemed to think I'd be able to manage it sooner rather than later, but I only have Rasila and Miar to help me now and who knows how long it'll take?

Mason stepped out of the hallway and slid his arms around her waist. "Is everything okay? He hasn't declared war on all toddler bullies or something, right? Or blew a raspberry that sent a kid through a wall with its sheer power?"

She laughed. "Brownstones don't go looking for trouble, you know. We merely end it when it comes looking for us. Anyway, I think it'd be hard for him to beat anyone up yet unless a little drool can take them out."

"You don't go looking for trouble?" Mason asked.

"No, I don't."

"You run a security company. Isn't looking for trouble kind of in the job description?"

"That's still not looking for it, only taking care of it." She folded her arms and nodded, a slight smile on her face. "You could argue that when I did bounty hunting, I was looking for trouble."

He kissed the back of her head. "I suppose it is more that it likes to come looking for your family, but given everything your dad did after Thomas was born, I doubt anyone dangerous or even a bully will get within one hundred yards of your brother for a long time. From what he told me the other day, there's even been a decrease in certain types of organized crime because all the groups are too busy trying to make sure no one does anything stupid."

Alison nodded. "Dad does have a way with intimidation. It doesn't help him much at the restaurant, but it's probably why his house has only been blown up once."

"Intimidation? Like forcing all the heads of LA's organized crime groups to attend his wedding and give him gifts?"

"I don't think he technically required them to give gifts. That was mostly them showing their respect." She laughed. "Many of them were interesting people, to be honest." She nodded at the baby. "But he makes you think, doesn't he?" She tugged out of her fiancé's hold and turned to grin at him. "The baby that is."

"Think what?" He offered her a playful smile.

"About having a kid," she teased.

Mason stared at her, a serious look on his face. "Fine. Let's do it."

She gaped.

Well, that backfired.

"Uh," she began. "I...time...place."

He burst out laughing. "Oh, A, you are so easy to mess with sometimes, it's almost not any fun." He grinned. "In all seriousness, it wouldn't be so bad and it's definitely something for the future, but I do think we should at least get our wedding planned before we move on to kids."

Alison crept closer to the bassinet. Shay had instituted a firm rule—those who wake the baby, deal with the baby. Mom herself was now taking her own nap. His sleep patterns had begun to stabilize, but it wasn't like he allowed his mother a solid night's rest and she had chosen to avoid any potions until he switched to solid foods. Thomas didn't respond much to laughs and talking around him, but brushing against his bassinet would wake him in an instant. James claimed it was an innate Brownstone tactical defensive instinct. His only defense would be trying to gum someone to death, of course, but Alison wouldn't put it past him.

"He smiled at me the other day," she murmured. "When I was doing this." She raised a hand and conjured a small image of a happy puppy. It ran a few feet in the air before it vanished.

"I'm not an expert on babies, but I'm reasonably sure that was probably only him passing gas." Mason shrugged, his expression playful.

"Maybe. Killjoy." She crouched beside the bassinet to stare while the tiny onesie-clad boy inside took his soft breaths. He was so peaceful, she was almost jealous. She looked at Mason. "Have you sensed any magic from him?"

He shook his head. "Nope. Why, have you?"

"No. I was simply curious."

"Why would you sense magic from him? Even if he has the potential, it wouldn't likely show up for a long time. But, more to the point—not to stress your adoption, A— but your current parents don't have true magical potential. Your dad's abilities are impressive, but they're technological. Advanced technology far beyond this planet's capabilities and even the Nine Systems Alliance's, but still science, not magic."

Alison stood and backed away. She now imagined baby Thomas tossing fireballs and summoning giant gumdrops, both for dropping on thugs and snacking. "The thing is, my dad is from a planet with no magic, and he grew up here and adapted to one with magic. It's not crazy that his son might somehow be capable of magic. You know. Genetics." Doubt crept into her voice at the end.

"I suppose stranger things have happened. Omni's a case in point, so your brother might have magic someday." Mason studied the baby. "But I think he has to master rolling over on his own at least before he worries about spells." He headed over to the couch and took a seat. "Although neither of your parents are full-time violent problem-solvers anymore, so maybe none of that will matter. I know things happened not all that long ago, but it wasn't like that person came to hurt them."

Alison wandered over to take a seat beside him. "Sure, but Dad's still obsessed with Thomas being trained from an early age." She shrugged. "And he had me training before I even had an artifact to help me see. The Brownstone definition of 'not ready to kick ass' is different than most normal people's—or even most not-so-normal people's. I sometimes forget that I'm the weird one."

"True enough." He leaned back and placed his arm around her shoulders. "While it's quiet and there are no dangerous parents around, we should talk."

"We are talking, or is that supposed to be code for something else?"

He snickered. "Nope. Talking is code for making noises with the help of our mouths. Specifically, I wanted to talk about the vacation and not your brother planking and doing boxing training as a toddler. Before you say something, helping your parents out with your newborn brother doesn't count as a vacation merely because it hasn't involved any gunfire. Not any gunfire past the first day, at least." He raised his other hand to cut her off when she opened her mouth to voice a protest. "He's adorable. There's no doubt about that, and I'm a big believer that family should be there for one another, but I am also a big believer in you having some relaxation. Every time your brother makes a strange noise, you freak out and grab two healing potions and prepare to cast healing magic."

She shook his arm off and huffed. "I don't do that, and you have to be careful. He's a baby. He might choke."

The life wizard smirked. "A, he only drinks milk right now."

"You can choke on milk." She frowned as she thought that through for a moment. "Or drown. Whatever you want to call it. The point is, babies are small and adorable but the trade-off is they are squishy, vulnerable, and can't kick much ass."

"Don't you think you're overreacting?" He raised a questioning eyebrow. "Thomas might have arrived early but he's healthy and a good weight. He's most likely healthier than a normal kid. And he has two solid parents who are obsessed with him, have access to magic, even if they can't cast it themselves, and are very, very wealthy." He gestured toward the bassinet. "If it comes down to it, Shay could hire an army of power English witch super-nannies. I bet Ava probably knows tons of them. I can see it now." He affected an English accent. "I knew them from back in the day. The King's Personal Seventh Arcane Super-Nanny Witch Brigade. I'd tell you more about them but if I did, the king would have me killed."

Alison chuckled. "She probably does." She uttered a

wistful sigh. "You're right. I am overreacting. I've always wanted a sibling, although it'll be weird having a brother who is so much younger than I am. Talk about a generation gap. I grew up in a world where magic was out in the open but there was still considerable separation. He'll grow up in a world where magicals are fully integrated into society and even cook barbecue."

"You do realize that most people don't place as much weight on barbecue as your father does, right?"

"Just saying."

"Sure." Mason shook a finger. "But you can't escape that easily."

"Can't escape what?"

"The vacation discussion," he clarified. "If I didn't know better, I'd say you didn't want to go on vacation."

"That's not true," she protested. "We were booked and ready to go. Life happened." She pointed at the baby. "He happened. Even if my dad wasn't off playing in Texas at the time, I would have to be here."

"I know. I'm not saying I didn't expect you to come, but I worry about you." He offered her a disarming smile. "I worry about all of us at the company. Hana wants to take a vacation too, you know."

"Then that's all the more reason for me to put things off for a while. She can go party with Tahir while we hold the fort down."

"Ah-ha!" A triumphant look settled over his face. "So you do want to avoid a vacation."

She groaned. "No, I only… It's not the right time."

"Hana won't go anywhere until you go first," he explained. "She told me that right before we left to come here. While she's doing that because she's your friend and cares about you, I'm willing to bet that if you ask Ava, there are other people in the company who might want to take vacations but don't want to because the Dark Princess sets an obsessive work example." He folded his arms and adopted a stern look. "Here's the thing. If I honestly believed you could actually let yourself relax here or at home, it'd be one thing, but you're always waiting for the other shoe to drop."

Alison shook her head. "Bomb, not shoe."

"The point is," he continued, admonishment in his tone, "that you need to go somewhere you can shut off one hundred percent. No checking in, no doing a quick call to an informant to see what the word is on who might show up. Then, and only then, will you be able to relax."

"But—"

"But nothing," Shay interrupted from the hallway, her tone sharp. She jabbed a finger in the air at her daughter. "You're done here." Her hair was a tangled mess and the fuzzy robe wasn't exactly the height of fashion. She was obviously focused on the practical reality of a newborn infant and not impressing guests, let alone family members.

She startled. "Mom?"

Mason smiled but kept his mouth shut.

"Consider this a parental order." Shay raised her chin, her "No Bullshit" face on full display. "It's been great having you here and I appreciate the break, but this isn't your kid. It's my kid, and I overheard enough to know that you'll tire yourself out even more to help me." She rolled her eyes.

"But Dad only took a couple of weeks off from the restaurant," Alison complained.

"Because I told him to go back," her mother explained. "He's been great—better than I expected, actually—but he sits there and stares at Thomas, and I know he's thinking about toddler assault courses and if the baby should wander around with Whispy on. You're so much like him. When you sit around and don't have too much to occupy your time, you start overthinking. The baby's sleeping well now and everything's stable."

Her expression softened. "I'll be honest, Alison. One of the reasons I wanted you both to stay was simply because some of the stuff spooked me a little." She looked to the side. "It's been a long time since I needed to protect someone who couldn't do a decent job of taking care of themselves, and it helped me relax to know your dad, you, and Mason were around, but everything's fine now. I'm not as worried, so it's time for you to go on with your life and take a vacation."

"There's no hurry," she assured her. "We missed the window on our reservation, so we could stay—"

"Come on, A," Mason admonished.

Shay nodded, her arms folded. "He's right. I'm telling you to go. You could simply call them and demand a spot anyway. You forget you're not merely some random woman. You're a celebrity."

"I want less attention, not more. Being the celebrity bitch won't help with that." She sighed and rested her head against the couch. "But it's not like we can't find somewhere else to stay."

"Exactly," he replied.

9

She stared at the ceiling and a slight frown came to her face. "But before we go, I think we should do something you and Dad can't."

"What's that?" the woman asked. "Go three days without eating meat?"

Alison straightened and rubbed her hands together. "You have artifacts sprinkled around and enough weapons in the house to start a war. You have enough artifacts and weapons in warehouses to win a war, but you aren't true magicals. I want to strengthen the wards on this place. Mason can help me. There are limits to what I can do since you and Dad won't be able to interact with them magically, but at least it's something more and it'll give me peace of mind."

Her mother glanced at Mason. "Is this her stalling again?"

He shook his head. "I'm sure we can get it done fairly quickly."

"There is one other thing I think you should do before you leave, though," Shay added with a thoughtful expression.

"What?" Alison asked.

"I need to get James fully grounded again," her mother explained. "He's happy to have a new kid and is adjusting well, but he's putting on a brave face. His little KISS world has been rocked and familiarity will help to restore it. That's another reason I told him to go back to work. But I think it'd help if you went on a bounty trip with him—something easy, so he can work out a little tension without going on another road trip. He could kick ass for a quick bounty rather than all that complicated crap like in Texas."

"That sounds fine."

Shay looked at Mason. "Only a father-daughter thing, okay?"

He nodded. "Understood."

Alison smiled. "It'll be fun to have something more straightforward than most of the stuff we've had to deal with in Seattle these past few months."

CHAPTER TWO

The next morning, Alison sat in the passenger seat of her dad's F-350 as they cruised along the highway on their way to the bounty target. She hadn't had much luck finding anything interesting, but James had awoken to an alert from a nice, juicy level-four who had rolled into town. Her dad contacted his people and had a possible location within an hour.

It's really strange that this is the kind of thing we do for bonding in this family, but everyone's different. Besides that, we don't even really need to do bounties ourselves anymore. Neither of us are danger fiends, either, yet this is our go-to when we want to de-stress.

She chuckled and shook her head.

James glanced briefly at her. "What's so funny?"

"I was thinking about how you have the agency and I have my company. We basically have armies we can call on command, complete with artifacts, anti-magic gear, and even magicals. If we added exoskeletons or power armor, they would be armies." She pantomimed firing a rifle. "The only reason the government isn't constantly up our asses is that we keep ourselves under control."

"So? We pay our employees well and like you said, we don't let them run wild. What's the problem?"

"It's only kind of funny when you think about it. At least it is to me." She shrugged. "I never thought when I met you years ago that either of us would end up being in charge of an army. Bounty hunting and security contracting weren't careers I ever remotely considered."

He grunted. "I'm not in charge of shit. I run the restaurant these days. Maria and the others take care of everything. She talks constantly about retiring, but it's been all these months and she still hasn't, so it might be something she talks about for the next ten years. It'll be annoying when she does, but I'm not one to tell someone they have to do something they don't want to do merely because it makes my life easier. Besides, it's not like she doesn't already have some half-decent replacements waiting."

"Whatever you say, Dad." She looked out the window at the stream of cars on the highway. Any one of them could contain a deadly bounty as a driver or passenger. She didn't always like having to constantly engage criminal elements—either as a bounty hunter or running a security company—but they now lived in a world where even the most normal-looking person could be dangerous in ways the most fanatical terrorist could have only dreamed about in decades past. The beginning of the opening of the gates had changed the world, and it was only a miracle that the chaos following the event hadn't destroyed Earth.

The police and government are finally starting to catch up. Maybe by the time Thomas is an adult, the idea of active anti-magic bounty hunters will be a weird thing people have a hard time even believing we ever allowed. I find it hard to believe that the police let Dad and I run around doing our thing.

She frowned when another thought intruded. There were more important things to discuss than their jobs.

"You and I haven't had a lot of time to talk one on one since the baby was born," she ventured.

"Yeah?" James shrugged. "What about the baby? He's fine, even if he constantly spits up on me."

"That's not what I'm getting at. Is everything okay with you? I know you're not exactly in touch with most of your feelings, but I'd like to be there for you if I can, Dad. There are ways to deal with things other than road trips and barbecues, and I get that you can't always talk to Mom about things."

He shook his head. "Shay told me to go on the last road trip, and it wasn't about barbecue. I only ate barbecue along the way."

"I know, I know. But this is a huge change. I don't know how I'd handle it." She tried her best to offer a comforting smile.

Her father changed lanes as their exit was only a few minutes away now. "Like I said, Thomas is good for a baby. He cries only when he needs something, and all the podcasts say his behavior is normal. I know he's different genetically and shit, but he's not turning orange and growing fangs or talking in full sentences already." His mouth twitched. "That's annoying, actually, but I'll deal with it."

Alison stared at him, confused. "You want him to be a

fanged, orange baby who talks in full sentences? I honestly don't understand you."

"No, not that. The opposite. Not the fucking fangs or color. You were already talking when I met you."

"I was a teenager, not a baby." She laughed. "I wasn't that unusual."

"That's my point. I didn't always get much of the emotional shit, but you could explain it to me. But Thomas? All he can do is cry. Yes, I know it's not supposed to be complicated. Usually, it only means he shit himself or he's hungry, but he's still so young. It's hard to know what he's really thinking. For all I know, he's not worried about that other stuff."

She laughed again. "He's a baby, Dad. He's not having deep existential thoughts. 'I could really go for some milk right now' and 'Where's Mom? She smells nice, and she has the best milk.'"

"You're right." He chuckled and changed lanes again to take the exit. "I'll let you know if I need to talk, but I'm good."

"I'm glad to hear that."

The next few minutes passed in silence until they pulled into the cracked parking lot of a U-shaped single-story dark building that might charitably be called a motel. Weeds waged a fairly successful campaign in the parking lot, and it looked like the faded and peeling walls hadn't been painted since before she was born. Surprisingly, there was a pool, although the only water present was mostly from the rain. Less surprisingly, algae choked it and basically left the recreational addition a West Nile factory. A drooling man sprawled against the wall, an empty baggie and syringe beside him.

Alison shook her head. "You know one thing I like about running a security company?"

"No." James patted his pockets to verify the presence of his potions and magazines. "Having a fancy building?"

"I don't only take rich clients, but no matter who I'm working for, they aren't total scumbags." She nodded at the hotel. "And so I don't have to come to places like this all that often, only when I need to make a point." She sighed. "Are you sure this is the right place? A level-four like our boy can probably afford something better than a roach motel."

He nodded. "Davion may be as annoying as fuck at times, but he's a good infomancer. If he says our guy's here, he's here. Room twenty-two."

"And you're sure about not having a direct link to Davion?" she asked.

Her father had briefly mentioned not being in direct contact before they set out.

"Yeah. This is supposed to be about bonding and shit, so we might as well make it old school. Before Davion, before Heather, and back to the very beginning when I didn't have an army." He slid his hand under his shirt and beneath the amulet to remove the spacer that separated it from his chest. His expression settled into a grimace for a moment before he breathed out slowly through his nose once the bonding was complete.

He's had that thing for so long and has all those mental conversations with it, but he still can't simply turn it on and off with a word. Maybe that's a good thing. It means he still knows where James Brownstone stops and where Whispy Doom begins.

Using the symbiont might be overkill with her there, but they were dealing with a level-four so it didn't hurt to be a little careful. Once magic was involved, things became unpredictable.

"Do you miss it?" Alison gestured at the motel.

"Miss shitty motels?" James scratched his cheek and wrinkled his brows. "I've never really been a fan."

"No, I mean bounty hunting full-time. I know you like running the restaurant, but I didn't know if it was enough excitement for you."

"Excitement's overrated." He rumbled a laugh. "But all the recent shit these last few months shows me something I already knew."

"What's that?"

He opened his door and stepped out of the truck. "That it's a good idea to remind everyone who I am now and again so they don't get any ideas. Maybe I haven't done it enough."

She opened her door, her eyes narrowed. Without thought, she sniffed the air—a horrible mistake given the plethora of fetid odors that hung in the area. "I sense a decent amount of magic around here, Dad. Is this some kind of halfway house for magical criminals? Or only the Swarm?"

"The Swarm. Fuck." James grimaced.

"Jai Talmidge. It's his nickname. That's what you told me."

"Yeah. But it's stupid. Hearing you say it aloud only

reminded me of how fucking stupid it is." He grunted and muttered something under his breath.

The morning's bounty wasn't a true magical. He had managed to get his hands on an ancient pendant that allowed him to create and control magical bugs. It had allegedly been corrupted by an unscrupulous ancient Greek Tithonus cult that experimented with dark magic. The artifact's enchantment also complicated straightfor-ward magical tracking, but Davion was able to locate the man with a combination of hacking and drones. It wasn't quite as "old-fashioned" as it could be in terms of their bonding trip, but it did save the Brownstones considerable time.

James resumed the conversation after a few moments' thought. "I suppose 'Swarm' makes sense since he has the stupid artifact that lets him do bug magic and shit, but the guys with nicknames are always the most obnoxious. We'll be lucky if he doesn't make us listen to a stupid speech, and he's not a dead-or-alive so we can't simply kill him to shut him up."

"Nicknames are stupid? Like the Dark Princess and the Granite Ghost?" Alison smirked.

He shrugged. "If we were bounties, we'd be level-five or -six and we'd be fucking annoying."

"I do like to give speeches," she admitted. Her smirk turned into a mask of disgust. "I keep thinking about how the bounty notice said he's basically a one-man budget mercenary army since he can make huge bugs."

"Big bugs squish exactly like small bugs." He crushed a nearby cockroach under his bootheel to illustrate his point.

"It's not a big deal. He's only a level-four, but at least this will be worth our time."

"I know." She shuddered and gestured to his boot. "I've fought my share of giant bugs—including giant cockroaches—but that doesn't make them any less disgusting." She closed her eyes and raised her hands to layer a few shields over herself. Although she'd worked on shadow healing with the help of Rasila and Miar, it wouldn't do her any good if someone surprised her with a headshot. She frowned and looked around. "And you're sure the guy can't discern magic himself? I don't like how much magic I can sense." She pointed past the algae-filled mess toward the other side of the building. "Both there." She gestured above them. "And some from up there. Maybe Davion tipped him off somehow."

"That could be, but if you still sense the magic, it means he has to be here." James surveyed the area slowly, his hand inside his coat and resting on the grip of his pistol. "But I don't remember anything about the guy being able to sense magic."

Alison narrowed her eyes and tilted her head to stare into the sky. Small dark shapes fluttered where the magic seemed to be concentrated. "Oh, shit."

"What?"

She sighed. "Moths. There is a...okay, I'm not sure what to call them, so let's go with a swarm of magical moths circling the motel."

He lowered his hand and retrieved his phone from his pocket. In silence, he brought up the bounty notice and scrolled through it quickly. "Fuck. I guess I should have read the whole thing."

"Meaning what?" she asked, her tone tight.

"It says in here he can use conjured bugs as living spy cameras and shit."

"Which means he's already seen two famous bounty hunters and a famous bounty hunter's truck," she observed. "So much for surprise."

Her father seemed unperturbed. "Shit happens."

"Why didn't you read the whole thing?"

"He's only a level-four and I've been distracted with the baby and shit."

"It's fine, I guess. The damage is done and he knows we're here." She funneled magic into her hand and formed a shadow blade. "That makes it easy in that we don't have to worry about clever tricks."

"I don't like doing sneaky shit with bounties," James replied, a faint hint of irritation in his eyes. "We're in the parking lot and you can sense his stupid bug magic. If he tries to run, you can simply follow him. So, let's go kick his door in. If he's not a total fucking moron, he'll surrender."

"Kick his door in?"

"I'll pay for it. Let's do this shit before he gets any stupid ideas." He turned toward the motel. "This might even be easier now that he knows we're here. He's probably pissing himself."

Alison kept pace with her father and strolled casually beside him like they were window shopping in a mall despite the speckled energy field that surrounded her body and the tenebrous magical blade in her hand. "Why do you assume it's easier to not have surprise?"

"Because we're not two random dumbasses," James explained. "We're the Brownstones. I know you've convinced people to surrender merely by telling them who you are."

"Yeah, I have, and so have you, but they don't always, right?" she replied. "Sometimes, people are stubborn idiots."

"Shit. Let's hope we're lucky today."

Loud, shrill fire alarms shrieked. Birds fled the roof of the building and several people threw their doors open and ran.

Huh. They have good emergency instincts.

A few fleeing guests noticed the Brownstones, screamed, and bolted in the opposite direction.

Father and daughter slowed to a stop while dozens of people, many half-dressed, emerged from their rooms. For such a questionable establishment, they did brisk business, but she wasn't sure how much of that was hourly given the look of a few panicked men and women who sprinted away.

"Do you see him?" she asked and her gaze scanned the evacuees hastily. "There are too many people."

James growled in annoyance. "Let's push on to the room." He jogged forward and the crowd parted for him and streamed past on either side. A few glanced at him with fear in their eyes.

Alison rushed after her father and darted between the fleeing people. They didn't give her as much of a wide berth as they did James, but no one came too close either. It was more evidence for her criminal hideout theory.

He arrived at the door to room twenty-two. The curtains were closed but the smoke alarm shrieked its unpleasant tune, the original source of the system-wide activation. To her surprise, he knocked. The door moved a few inches.

"Fuck," he muttered.

She caught up with him. "I don't sense any magic from inside." She concentrated and looked up. "And I hate to tell you this, Dad, but I don't sense it up there either. Unless he starts using considerable magic again, I won't be able to follow his trail directly."

He threw the door wide open. "Damn it."

A half-filled suitcase lay on the rumpled bed, along with a plate of pad thai with a plastic fork half-buried in the noodles. Acrid smoke filled the room, and a charred mess that looked like the remains of burned paper and plastic rested inside the blackened interior of a microwave.

"I hate it when they have even half a brain," she muttered and released the magic that fueled her blade. "Either he saw us coming and purposefully started a fire..." She pointed to the smoke alarm. "Or he's played with bugs too long and had some creative ideas about dessert."

"I'll call Davion, I guess." James gritted his teeth. "It was supposed to be a quick bounty."

"Don't worry." Alison walked toward the bathroom. "I have an idea. We can still track him."

"The bounty notice said basic tracking wouldn't work."

"Well then, it's a good thing I'm not limited to that." She stopped at the sink, looked down, and retrieved a single dark hair. "Let's hope this is his hair because I doubt that he can stop a direct tracking spell."

"This shit is already annoying," he grumbled. "Plus, remember this guy isn't a dead-or-alive, so we're gonna have to be careful when we catch up with him."

She laughed. "Are you getting a little lazy, Dad?"

"Barbecue doesn't involve weird-ass insects, only the occasional magic pineapple cow."

"Are you still bitching about that?" She found a paper cup and half-filled it with water, raised her palm, and chanted a quiet spell. A small needle appeared. "It's time to show bug man what real magic's about."

He grinned. "Complicated and as annoying as shit?"

She smiled in response. "Much of the time, yes."

CHAPTER THREE

Alison stared at the needle in her cup. "Take the next right, Dad."

Her direct tracking spell worked without any difficulty. Unless the Swarm managed to put significantly more distance between himself and the Brownstones, he would have to deal with a vexed father-daughter team in LA within minutes.

James tightened his hands around the wheel as he complied. "I'll tell you what doing these kinds of thing helps with. It makes me appreciate how even shitty barbecue isn't that annoying."

"Another right." Her heart rate kicked up. "It's swinging so much now that he has to be close. Damned close."

When the F-350 made its next turn, she no longer needed the tracking spell nestled in the paper cup in the console holder. She could sense the intense magic from a beat-up Hyundai coupe only a few car lengths ahead of them.

"That's our boy," she declared. "Roach motel and a car

that looks almost as old as your truck. He needs to up his crime game."

"My F-350 doesn't look like a piece of shit," he insisted.

"I know. I know. I'm just saying."

He snorted dismissively but it had an edge of humor. "We need to get him off the road before he decides to turn this into a high-speed chase."

The driver's head turned for a moment, but he didn't accelerate or change direction abruptly despite clearly being able to see the huge truck. Instead, he continued to simply cruise along at the speed limit.

"What the fuck is his game?" her father muttered.

"I don't know," Alison replied. "He probably has another trick in store."

They followed the Hyundai for a few blocks. The bounty pulled into the mostly empty parking lot of a grocery store and Alison's stomach tightened.

I'm glad we did this so early in the morning.

The vehicle rolled to a stop and the emaciated Talmidge emerged from the car, an ornate bronze pendant hung around his neck. He stretched a hand out and splayed his fingers.

James slammed the brakes on about ten yards away. "If that fucker messes my truck up, I'll feed him to his fucking bugs in pieces."

She raised her hands, ready to cast more shield spells, but no attack erupted from the bounty's hand.

Talmidge waved with his other hand but kept the first outstretched.

The Brownstones exited the F-350, their attention locked on their target.

"Jai Talmidge," James bellowed. "You have a level-four bounty. I'm not gonna waste time saying anything else. Do you want to fight us? Go ahead. We'll simply kick your ass and you'll go to the hospital first and then jail. Actually, fuck that. You'll go to jail all busted up. Why not cut out a few steps?"

"Brownstone and daughter," Talmidge shouted in response. "I'm almost honored that both of you needed to come and capture me."

"Don't get too big a head," she replied and extended a shadow blade. "This is merely our version of a Sunday picnic or mini-golf."

The man looked confused for a moment and glanced from one to the other. "Huh?"

"We don't need to explain shit to you, Talmidge," her father grumbled. "Excuse me. The Swarm."

Dad's improved his sarcasm considerably these last few years.

"Fuck you, Brownstones." The bounty licked his lips. "You'd better leave me alone or I'll unleash six-legged hell. You think you're tough but I'm not simply a random little bitch you can push around. If you're here after me, you know I can hurt people." His hand began to glow a dull red. "I won't go to prison, and you won't make money off me. So, I'll give you the choice to get in your truck and drive the fuck away."

Alison shook her head and sighed. "I hate it when they're stubborn." She channeled energy into a spell and murmured an incantation. A streaming red flare streaked skyward.

"What the fuck is that?" their adversary yelled, his eyes wide.

"It's not an attack, asshole. Calm down." She rolled her eyes. "After all that posturing, you're now freaking out."

The flare exploded and crackled like a spectacular July Fourth rocket. Bright red letters lingered in the sky to form a message for everyone to read from miles around.

BROWNSTONE CAPTURE IN PROGRESS. PLEASE AVOID AREA.

"Huh." James drew his gun. "That's handy."

She smiled. "I imagine it'll also give us a few extra minutes before AET bothers to show up since they know it's us."

The trick might not work as well in Seattle, but her father had tamed the LA AET years earlier despite their initial distrust. A few people emerged from the grocery store and looked up. A couple immediately raced away. Another man retreated inside, waved his arms, and shouted—probably a warning to the occupants to get the hell out of there.

Talmidge gritted his teeth. "Just because a few idiots run away doesn't mean I can't hurt people. I can flood this whole area with my monsters. You can win against a few individuals but you can't win against the Swarm."

Alison looked at her father. "Do you think he practices that in the mirror?"

"Probably." He rumbled a laugh. "I told you—annoying speeches."

Employees and customers poured out of the store and all sprinted away from the parking lot.

She pointed her blade at Talmidge. "Come on. You've already lost. You couldn't win against one of us so there's no way you could win against both. All you're doing is wasting our time and earning yourself pain."

The bounty flung his arm up. "Fine. Don't beg for mercy when the time comes."

James snorted and fired once, his gun aimed at the bounty's leg. The bullet bounced off an inch from the man with a spark. "Huh. The bounty notice didn't mention that. It must be new." He holstered his weapon and retrieved a small cracked piece of glass, slipped it under his shirt, and pressed it against his amulet.

Alison didn't need to see what was going on to understand that her father was feeding a magical artifact to his symbiont for power. A few seconds later, a biometallic layer covered his right arm and a sharp blade extended.

"Are you not going full coverage?" she asked.

"It depends on whatever this fuck has in mind," he replied.

Energy blasted from Talmidge but vanished after a few yards. Red twisting streams erupted from the ground and surrounded the man. He sneered in defiance. "You had your chance."

The flows formed into a mass of large ants and spiders, each a few yards in length, their dark eyes magnified. Their clicking mandibles dripped with a viscous green fluid that sizzled and burned the asphalt on contact, leaving small indentations.

"You know..." She shook her head. "I somehow expected them to be bigger." She gestured widely with her hands. "Like as big as a car. I'm kind of disappointed, actually. But pony-size is kind of scary, I guess."

"Yeah. I know what you mean." James lifted his blade.

"It only said 'giant bugs' in the notice." Armor strands ejected from his amulet to coat everything but his head with shielding. His pants and shirt ripped, and his holster fell. "I'm a bounty hunter, not an exterminator."

"Are you mocking me?" Talmidge screamed.

"We're mocking your bugs, actually," she clarified. "But that could be interpreted as mocking you, I suppose." She shunted magical energy into her legs. Sometimes, a woman should use wings and sometimes, she merely needed a nice boost. "But, yeah, I'm not impressed. They're more gross than terrifying."

"Now we have to get the stupid pendant off him," her father stated. "Otherwise, these fucking bugs will run around for hours."

"That's right," Talmidge thundered and backed away. "You'll regret this."

The ants and spiders skittered forward, a chittering, clacking mass of limbs, fiery eyes, and dripping acid.

"This is not how I imagined my morning going," she muttered.

CHAPTER FOUR

When the disgusting bugs scuttled toward them, Alison released her stored leg energy and launched herself forward. She whipped her blade to the side and sliced through an ant along the way. The gaping wound showered green fluid that sizzled when it made contact with the asphalt and the conjured monster collapsed. She barreled into a spider and an overhead slash cleaved easily through her arachnid opponent and left it in two pieces.

Huh. This proves I don't have any bug phobias, but this is still disgusting. What's next? We have to take on the Rat King?

An ant rushed forward and tried to snare her with its mandibles. The bite bounced off her shield and she removed the creature's head. A moment of relief passed through her when the body collapsed.

Oh, wait. It's cockroaches that can run around without heads. I hope this guy doesn't alter their abilities.

Ants spat acid at James. The globs landed all over his body but slid down with little noticeable effect. Even a splash against his exposed face only summoned a grunt and reddened his cheek. The discoloration faded a few seconds later. He marched forward with no particular urgency and swiped at the first beast that launched itself at him. An enemy fell with each step as he pierced its body or dismembered it.

Alison tried to close on Talmidge, but a surge of twitching legs and mandibles blocked her path. She generated another blade and hacked furiously with all the precision of a crazed woman using a machete in a dense jungle. One strike separated a mandible and another removed legs. Others halved heads or bodies. The acidic blood of the magical bugs fell around her, seared the ground, and forcing her to channel more magic into her shields.

I bet this is way more frustrating for other bounty hunters.

"Okay, this is starting to go from annoying to disgusting," she yelled.

"At least they aren't saying shit," her father replied. He continued his ponderous advance and left a trail of twitching bodies in his wake. Three ants attacked him together, but their vicious bites and acid left only the faintest scratches on his armor. His regeneration erased the minor victories within seconds, and his counterattacks shredded them like they were made of tissue.

He slammed his foot into an approaching spider. Its head collapsed with a loud crunch, and the body tumbled for several yards before it landed and pinned a squirming ant.

"No, no, no," Talmidge yelled, his face tight. Now, both his hands were cloaked in a nimbus of magical energy.

"What? Do you have another speech?" James demanded.

"Fine," the other man replied. "I'll flood this whole neighborhood with my creations if necessary."

Another pulse surged from the bounty. Dozens of giant wasps appeared in twisting streams of red energy, along with spider and ant reinforcements.

Sweat poured down Talmidge's face, and even at distance, his ragged breathing was easy to see.

So you're pushed to your limit, huh?

Alison leapt high, released her blades, and grew shadow wings. Without hesitation, she shoved her palms out and released bright bolts of light magic. They streaked away and struck the heads of two wasps. The creatures fell, charred and very dead.

Dad can handle all the ground clean-up, but I can't let any of these things escape.

She spun to continue her attacks and targeted the farthest wasps as they buzzed away. A solid strike to a wing or body was sufficient to eliminate them. None of them retaliated despite the charred bodies of their kin.

James continued his inexorable advance toward Talmidge. She half-wondered if he enjoyed intimidating the bounty. The ants and spiders concentrated their assaults on him, unlike the wasps. One flying creature cleared the parking lot before Alison seared both its wings off. It fell to the road and narrowly missed a brave motor-cyclist who had ignored the large red warning in the sky.

We need to finish this before it gets out of hand.

Her focus returned to the swarm and she hovered in place and spun as she flung wave after wave to annihilate the insect air force. A huge pulse of magic forced her atten-tion to Talmidge and she did a double-take. A giant cocoon, easily over ten feet, now stood where he had been before. Magic pulsed from it every few seconds. She jerked her head up and seared another wasp that thumped into the roof of the grocery store with a sickening crunch.

I hope the bodies disappear after a few hours and it's not simply that they die. I'd hate to be part of the clean-up crew.

A throbbing mass of angry insects buried James in a concerted push for supremacy. A few seconds later, most of them hurtled away in various directions as he thrust out with his arms and legs. The few survivors didn't last much longer against his methodical extermination—fueled, of course, by his irritation.

Alison took quick breaths as her rapid-fire aerial anni-hilation continued. The flying swarm became a mere group under the concentrated hostile light magic. The creatures thudded and crunched onto the surface like a hard but somewhat soggy rain. The group soon became a few individuals. Finally, the last wasp plummeted to the parking lot, already dead with a hole in its head and a missing wing.

Below, her father had thinned the crawling horde, but sheer numbers kept him away from the cocoon. She circled the parking lot and took a few moments to concentrate magic into her attacks before she launched them into the rear of the frenzied insects. Her white-blue orbs exploded and shredded the outer ring while he continued to methodically punch, kick, and slice. He even headbutted one spider and caved its head in.

How much does it cost to repair a parking lot? It's a good thing this is a level-four bounty.

The combined air and ground assault destroyed the

remaining bugs in less than a minute. Carcasses, detached and twitching dark chitinous limbs, and pools of acid now coated the asphalt. The deadly liquid ate the tattered lower remnants of James' pants, but whatever damage they inflicted to his armor didn't occur rapidly enough to offset its repair.

Alison floated down to her father but remained a few inches above the ichor-covered ground. "That was interesting. I'm still on the fence about whether it was fun, though."

He pointed at the cocoon beyond the shallow acid pools. "What's up with that?"

"Maybe he'll come out a giant butterfly?" she joked. "I'd blast right through it, but I risk killing the guy."

James shook his head. "Nah. He won't go anywhere if he's hiding in there." He pointed to a few police drones that circled in the distance. "The cops are watching. AET might already be on the way. They can bust him open if he wants to hide."

The cocoon shuddered.

"I don't think he plans to wait," she observed and shook her hands out before she wiped the sweat away from her forehead. After a deep breath, she conjured a new shadow blade. "He might have simply been healing or restoring his energy in there. Did the bounty say anything about that?"

The cocoon ripped down the center and a jointed dark-green leg several yards long emerged, followed seconds later by two more.

"Seriously? You have to be kidding me," she muttered.

A gargantuan cicada emerged from the sheath. A bright crimson glow suffused his eyes.

"What the hell?" Her father grimaced and shook his head in disbelief.

"Of course." She shrugged. "Cult of Tithonus."

"I'm not Shay. What's that supposed to mean?"

"It's a Greek myth. There are various versions of the how and why, but in many of them, a guy named Tithonus is turned into an immortal cicada." She elevated a few feet. "Like so much crap from the past, the myth apparently had some basis in fact."

He grunted. "That must have been what they meant by extreme regeneration and shapeshifting potential in the bounty notice."

The giant cicada shook his head and bared his flaming fangs.

"At least it only has one head," James commented. He uttered a low growl. "Hey, Talmidge. This shit's already been annoying. If you still have your mind in there, you should simply surrender. I need you alive so I don't lose the bounty and have to pay for all the repairs myself."

Talmidge stomped forward before he stopped several yards from his adversary. If he were capable of speech, he didn't demonstrate it.

"You should have turned into a dragonfly and flown away," Alison suggested. "But we tracked you once and can do it again. If it was only one of us, maybe you might have had a chance to get away, but both of us? You should have saved everyone's time and surrendered from the beginning. Now, because of you, there's a big mess someone has to clean up."

His wings came to life. He didn't lift off but the force of his flapping splashed acid and the remains of his army into an insect-parts storm that blinded both Brownstones for a moment. Talmidge leapt into the air, his flight pattern uneven and clumsy as he flew away.

"No, you don't." She surged in pursuit and caught up to him up after only a few seconds. A few quick slices removed the wings, and a twirling mid-air kick launched the rest of the new insect in an arc toward her father. The bounty hunter lunged to meet the approaching giant cicada and severed three legs. The target thudded to earth and half his new body cracked and twisted on impact. James pivoted and launched himself forward while Alison flew toward the bounty.

"I think that might have been too much," she suggested and her father paused and looked at her.

Red light spread from the cicada's eyes to engulf the rest of his body, the intensity blinding. It died a moment later to reveal a human Talmidge on the asphalt, naked except for the bronze pendant. His arms and legs lay at extreme angles and lacerations covered his flesh.

We cut off all the extras, but everything he needs is still there. He's still breathing, too.

He jerked and twitched and his twisted limbs rotated into their original position. His wounds began to seal while he pushed himself to his feet where he stood a moment, swayed, and spat blood.

"That's kind of annoying." Alison scowled.

"I'm...not...finished," the bounty wheezed. "You... haven't...won."

James grunted. "Fuck you. Honestly, you're really starting to piss me off now."

"Let's end this, shall we?" She flew toward the man and

swung her blade—not at his body but at the chain holding the pendant. The tip severed a link, which sparked briefly before the artifact fell. She held the blade to his neck. He raised his hands and fell to his knees, half his wounds still open.

"I surrender!" he cried.

"See, that wasn't so hard was it?" She smiled. "Now, we wait for the police."

Her father kicked a few spider carcasses out of the way. "You know what? I do feel more relaxed. Shay was right."

She nodded. "Now that it's all over, I've changed my opinion. This was fun. Gross, but fun, and I'll have a funny story to tell on vacation."

CHAPTER FIVE

A couple of days later, Alison shook her hands out as she jogged down a ramp in the multi-level structure created in her tactical training room. She studied the half-melted rails and debris spread around. "I knew we should have done this in the middle of nowhere. I knew you two would cut loose but I didn't expect it to be this bad."

Two shadow-winged Drow descended from either side of the room.

"It was your suggestion," Rasila reminded her with a smirk as she landed. "Although I did find your techno-magic threats interesting."

"You're right. I suggested it and I control the building, and none of my employees blink at the idea of me telling them to stay out of this room for an hour. I don't always want to destroy a random location, even if it is in the middle of the wilderness." She looked around and snorted as she focused on a collapsed bridge. "It was merely rougher than I anticipated."

"I can see the appeal of this kind of training environment, and your subordinates must find it very useful. They probably have fewer issues with extensive damage."

Miar settled on the ground and her wings vanished. Her normally gleaming black armor was dull and cracked. She sheathed her sword, having an actual physical weapon unlike the other two. "True threats have souls. I'm dubious of this kind of training, but if you find it useful, it doesn't hurt me to aid you on occasion." She gestured toward the collapsed bridge. "But repair magic will help with the other problem. The three of us and your subordinates will be able to handle it."

"There can be issues with repair spells and technomagic components," Alison explained. "But like Rasila said, it was my suggestion. Don't worry about it. I suppose Myna was always a little more careful than I realized." She retrieved a water bottle stashed near the wall and downed its contents before she turned to the two Drow princesses. "It's nice to spar and it's nice to remind myself of what a Drow princess is capable of in a fight, but we've focused more on that kind of thing during the last sessions. That said, I think your continued help with shadow compression is more useful. It's the only way I'll be able to portal."

"I thought you were a little frustrated the last time we attempted portaling," Rasila replied. "I was the one who suggested to Miar that we focus only on fighting this time." She pointed to Alison. "Although your shadow healing is better, you still have room for improvement."

She nodded, a little surprised by an unexpected realization.

I let Rasila convince me to drop my shield so she could stab me for the test. What the hell? Do I trust her that much? When did that happen?

She glanced at Miar.

Or do I trust Miar that much?

They respect strength. I might not have mastered all my abilities, but I'm strong, even compared to them, and much younger.

In all honesty, she wasn't sure. She didn't have any defenses up at that moment. Either Drow princess could throw a rapid attack and stun her long enough for a follow-up. Miar could use her enchanted sword. Somewhere along the line, training and mutual information-sharing had turned into something approaching a genuine friendship with the two Drow princesses.

Miar frowned. She raised her hand and whispered a spell. Purple-black light consumed her armor. The cracks, holes, and dings repaired themselves, and the light faded. "I think there's a different issue here, especially after seeing your progress on shadow healing, and it won't be something so easily resolved with simple training."

Rasila rubbed her chin. "I agree. With your power level and mastery of shadow compression, you should already be able to open portals—at least on this planet and at modest ranges. I'll admit to being puzzled by your inability to do so."

Alison shrugged. "I don't know what to tell you. I can't do it. I thought Myna meant I'd be able to master it eventually with enough shadow compression training, but she did have a habit of not always telling me everything I might want to know right away. Although she didn't seem to think I would ever have true natural Drow shapeshifting abilities, I can do many spells that accomplish the same thing so I'm not all that worried about it."

"Mindset," Miar insisted. She brushed a few stray white hairs out of her eyes. "There's something about your mixing of the light and shadow magic that, when combined with your focus, inhibits you. I believe it's different than shapeshifting. Most powerful magicals can open portals. That magic, for a Drow, isn't tied so directly to their fundamental nature. Your other failure feels odd given your power level and the other spells you are able to cast. If you lacked capability in other complex enchantments, that might explain it."

Rasila walked over to retrieve her key fob and purse. Natural Drow shapeshifting might let her fake a human appearance but conjuring a luxury car from thin air was more difficult and unlike Miar, she cared about fitting in on Earth. "If you're to have any chance at the throne, you'll need that ability, Alison. The Drow will never follow a queen who hasn't demonstrated mastery of her magic."

"That's not why I care," she replied. "I don't care about the throne. I thought that was clear by now."

"So you say. But that might change in the future and it's something you should keep in mind."

"I train with you because I need to get stronger and, to be blunt, because you two let me know what's going on with the Drow. That way, I don't end up blindsided by all this—kind of like I was with you. I have enough going on with people on Earth that I can't afford to be dragged into something dangerous on Oriceran without proper preparation."

Rasila's amused smile faded into a slight frown. "Ah,

then there is something I should share with both of you before we part ways. I meant to relate it earlier but I was excited about the battle. Forgive me."

Alison folded her arms. "What's going on?"

"My people have passed along some recent interesting information. Drae has attempted to consolidate the support of various factions. She's made it clear that she doesn't support Laena and has reiterated her dislike of the Guardians. It's clear now that she will make a direct claim to the throne."

"Is that really a surprise?"

"Suspecting something is different than knowing it, and confirmation that she will seek the throne for herself means that Novati is the only princess left who might possibly support Laena. Things are accelerating, Alison. I know you emphasize that you don't care, but you are involved, whether you want to be or not." Rasila looked to the side, an unfamiliar expression on her face—concern. "I trust in your power but growing up on Earth hasn't prepared you for the true struggle against other Drow."

Miar nodded her agreement, a stern look on her face. "Laena's corruption and cruelty led to laziness. That's what made it so simple for your father to handle her in the manner he did. Not all your foes will fall so easily."

"I understand all that." Alison sighed. "And you don't quite get it. It's not that I don't care. It's that I don't want to be queen. I'm trying to stay out of this, but Drow princesses keep showing up. Maybe I'll get lucky and Drae and Novati will be as reasonable as you two." She frowned at Rasila. "If I consider faking a job to ambush me reasonable."

The woman smirked, her normal façade restored. "No one died, so what's the point of complaining?"

Miar glowered. "Drae is a manipulative coward. You can't trust her. Even if she claims she is willing to give you aid, she will betray you. Novati is arrogant and ruthless. She lacks honor. I have no right to tell you what to do, but they will not be new allies for you, even if you approach them in the spirit of honor and open strength."

Rasila cleared her throat. "There's another issue with Drae."

"What?" Alison asked.

"She's specifically mentioned not liking your involvement in any part of this process. Basically, she considers you a human pretending to be a Drow. She's made it clear that she will not support any claim you have to the throne."

"So it's a good thing I don't want the throne, then." She rolled her eyes. "Does that mean I can look forward to this bitch showing up and challenging me to a duel?"

Miar scoffed. "Drae would never do something so bold and direct and will hide in the shadows and send minions to harass you. She is more assassin than warrior. In this, she reminds me of the Widowmaker." She sneered, the disdain written clearly on her face.

"That's a cheery thought." Alison kicked at the floor with her boot. "I'm supposed to go on a pleasant, relaxing vacation, and now you're saying I have to worry about Drow assassins?"

"I doubt she'll attempt to kill you directly. Murdering a princess is beneath her, and she understands the implications. Going so far would weaken her reign from the beginning." Miar's face tightened. "And if she made such a mistake, I'll ensure that she won't live long to regret her mistake."

"Thanks." She chuckled. "It's always good to know someone has sworn bloody vengeance on my behalf."

"That doesn't mean she's above killing those close to you," Rasila clarified. "Be cautious, but I doubt she's so eager that she'll plan to engage you or your people anytime in the near future. I only offer this as a warning."

"If all this Drow crap continues, I'll simply find some random Light Elf and support her for queen," Alison muttered.

Rasila and Miar winced.

CHAPTER SIX

Alison opened the door and stepped into the Brownstone Security pet park. She laughed when she spotted Hana kneeling in the center of the room to scratch a brown rooster behind the neck. He stood with his head tilted down and his feathers fluffed and uttered a quiet noise that might be called a coo, as incongruous as that was.

"Is this the first time Omni's been a rooster?" Alison asked. "I don't think I remember anyone even picking rooster for the pool but sometimes, I catch myself thinking he's been a certain type of animal and am not sure if I'm only imagining that."

Hana smiled at her. "He's been a rooster before but not at work. Is your princess playdate over?" She patted her alien pet one last time. He bobbed his head a few times before he wandered over to a cardboard tube, clucked enthusiastically, and pecked it.

It's weird to think that some alien super-intelligence might have ended up in the body of a creature who is now pecking cardboard tubes.

She snickered. "Yeah, Miar and Rasila are out of my hair for probably a month or two. Based on what they've told me, I'm probably courting a Drow invasion by hanging out with them, but it's hard to keep track of who wants to mess with me on any given week. It's like the bigger my rep gets, the greater the idiot who comes looking for trouble."

The fox stood and brushed the dust off the legs and knees of her hot-pink leggings. They didn't exactly strike her boss as screaming "security contractor," but arguably, neither did the jeans and T-shirt she'd changed into after she'd finished her training session. The company didn't have a formal dress code, and Ava actively advised against it citing, "the synergistic efficiency of tolerating individual employee idiosyncrasies." It wasn't like anyone wore crazy outfits on actual jobs.

"We've kicked more than a little ass," Hana replied and watched Omni continue to peck the cardboard tube and leave holes every few inches. "But I don't agree. The more we do, the more it convinces people not to mess with us. Otherwise, this building would be a crater. It's not like everyone doesn't know where it is, and the Seventh Order are the only ones who really tried to attack here. The Tapestry didn't send their corpse army at us even though they needed Omni to be the body of their big boss." She scoffed and rolled her eyes. "Losers."

Alison stared at the pet. "I'm kind of surprised. I always assumed he would talk at some point, but even though he's a wonder-pet, he's not actually shown that he's any smarter than a normal animal that doesn't change shape."

"My baby's fine exactly the way he is," the other woman insisted. "I have enough men talking in my life. Sometimes, you simply need an adorable baby who loves his Mommy and will rip out the throat of anyone who threatens her, even if they are a big, scary alien monster from another dimension."

Her boss laughed. "I remember when you were satisfied with the fish."

"That's only because you wouldn't let me have anything better." The fox gave her a stern look and put her hands on her hips. "I wanted an adorable furbaby from the beginning. It just so happens I got the ultimate pet. The universe rewarded my patience."

"That's one way to look at it."

Hana winked. "Everything in life comes down to how you look at it."

Omni moved on from his pecking and instead, wandered in a circle and made a faint noise reminiscent of a grunt.

Alison sighed. "I've been back a few days, and I've managed to fend Mason off for now, but he's still on me about the vacation."

Her friend laughed. "You say that like it's a bad thing. You were all ready to take a vacation before the baby was born."

"And it was planned and booked. I thought I had it all under control. Now, I'm not sure. He says we should take it easy, shut off completely, and disconnect, but there are still many different types of vacation. We could sit around in hammocks all day on one side or plan a schedule filled with sightseeing tours." She ran her tongue along the inside of her cheek as she pondered more possibilities. "The only thing I'm sure about is that I'm not leaving Earth."

"Why not?" Hana asked. "Visiting Oriceran would be interesting. The only time you've really gone there is for Drow training, right?"

She nodded. "That's the only significant amount of time I've spent there, yes."

"Then I don't understand the problem."

"There are too many risks. I might have magic and attended the School of Necessary Magic, but that's like saying someone's prepared to live in the US because they attended an extension college overseas. The truth is that I don't understand Oriceran well enough, and over here, I'm a licensed bounty hunter with a known security company. I have government contacts at city, state, and federal level. If I get into a battle over there, I might end up locked in a dungeon for violating some local noble's edict against fighting drunken pixies on a Saturday."

The fox laughed. "I'm sure that's not a law."

"Who knows? That's my point." Alison shrugged. "Not to mention that going over there makes me more of a target for Drow bullshit." She leaned against the wall. "Nope. I'm staying on Earth. If I'm supposed to relax, I want to relax, not fight off assassins or kill seven-headed demon badgers or insane gnome vampires."

"Gnome vampires? Is that really a thing?"

She snickered. "That's the problem with Oriceran. You never know. That's my point. I'm a Drow princess and you're a nine-tailed fox, and we're practically normal compared to some of the things over there. It's not a world where there is a little magic. It's a world where every single molecule is infused with intense magic. I suspect it's more alien, in many ways, than the planets of the Nine Systems Alliance."

Hana shook a finger. "Ignore Oriceran, then. I have the perfect solution. You should go on a vacation on Earth, but you shouldn't worry about sightseeing or doing anything that requires a schedule. Stay in bed with Mason all day except when you're eating, and make all the meals room service—no stress and no itineraries, only total relaxation. Honestly, you need to rest and prove to yourself you can do it before you consider your honeymoon."

"It's hard to relax when you're me," she countered. "I'm not trying to be a diva, but people always recognize me and then, I'm Alison Brownstone, the Dark Princess. The daughter of James Brownstone. Half-Drow who can fly, blah, blah, blah."

"Then go to a place where magicals aren't rare." Hana shrugged at her surprised look. "Yes, not everyone is as powerful as you, but if you're surrounded by people who live and breathe magic, they won't gawk as much."

"But I don't want to go to Oriceran. I told you that."

Her friend pointed dramatically to the floor. "Then find magical places on Earth."

She stared at her in confusion. "The pet park?"

Hana shook her head. "Just because it's bad in Seattle doesn't mean it's bad everywhere. Come on, Alison." She gestured impatiently at the floor again.

"A kemana?" She tilted her head and considered the

possibility. She hadn't even thought of them when she'd scheduled her previous vacation. "Fair enough, there will be mostly magicals there, but what's so restful about kemanas?"

With the beginning of the opening of the gates, the kemanas had lost some of their purpose. Most were towns built around massive crystal deposits that had been charged with magic in the distant past to provide energy to beings on Earth when the gates were closed. They also provided a refuge for those who would otherwise have been hunted on the surface in the time where the open use of magic was forbidden. In a sense, they became almost a parallel magical civilization hidden underground, a safe haven for Oriceran and Earth magicals alike.

While the full magical potential of Earth lay thousands of years in the future, the steady flow of magic from Oriceran to Earth now meant that most magicals didn't require the kemanas to recharge, although some species still had difficulty in the lower magical environment outside the kemanas. The chaos that made bounty hunters necessary was proof enough that the magic of the surface was sufficient to already change Earth.

"I read something the other day about a big boom in kemana tourism," the other woman explained. "It's a huge attraction these days. It's how the smaller ones are trying to make up for losing people to the surface cities or bigger kemanas near those places. Look into it. It's an idea." Excitement lit her face. "I'm considering a kemana resort trip myself, but I'm still working on convincing Tahir to unplug."

"Huh," she replied. "That's a good idea."

That evening, Alison lay in bed in silence beside Mason. He scrolled through some gallery pictures from the Louvre.

I wonder if he wants to go to France. I can see the appeal, but my recent track record with foreign countries points to me blowing up half of Paris and then having to explain to an elite French witch-hunting squad why I'm even there.

"I'm on the fence," she admitted. "I was all ready to go. You know I was, and I booked the trip."

He set his phone on his nightstand and sat, his exposed chest letting her soak in the sight of his muscles. For all his magic, he spent every day in the gym and the current show was proof enough of that. Good magic enhanced a strong body and made him a weapon.

I need to concentrate here.

"And why are you on the fence now?" He quirked a brow and a slight smile played across his lips. "I thought we worked this out, A. Thomas is fine. Your mom told you to go. You kicked ass with your dad, and we don't have any big assignments coming up that require either you or me. Ava even told me she's making sure of that."

"Sometimes, I wonder if we should change the name of the company, but I can't complain about having an ultra-competent assistant who could probably defeat a Drow princess if she really decided it was necessary." She groaned softly. "The whole situation with Drae has me worried. I know they said she wouldn't try anything soon, but they also said she might try to target people I care about."

"Everyone you care about can take care of themselves,"

he reminded her. He took her hand in his and squeezed. "If Drae targets your family, there will be one less Drow princess left alive to bid for the throne—and that's assuming your dad doesn't go Forerunner and destroy all the Drow."

Alison grimaced. Strictly speaking, she wasn't certain he could do that on his own, even at full power. At the same time, she couldn't ignore the possibility given what he'd already demonstrated on multiple occasions, including against groups like the Council and during the Battle of LA.

"My family aren't the only people at risk," she countered. "There's everyone in the company, too."

"Yes, your company, where most people here during the day are in a building probably better warded than King Oriceran's palace and almost every single person—aside from a handful of admin staff—is highly trained in self-defense and dealing with magical threats. Oh, and you have an entire armory filled with anti-magic deflectors and anti-magic bullets. You have a world-class infomancer with an apprentice who's better than most pro-infomancers, both of whom can indirectly control hordes of security robots. Not to mention a nine-tailed fox with dozens of artifacts and a sword that can cut through anything, and that's before we mention her pet when he gets angry."

"They are well-trained," she admitted reluctantly.

Mason rubbed her palm with his thumb. "And Tahir's always been paranoid. Remember, he's not that great in a fight but he still managed to eliminate a number of criminals when they attacked him at his old apartment. The Tapestry targeting Hana only strengthened that paranoia."

He frowned. "That reminds me. If we go offline, we need to make sure he disables all those automatic SOS systems he set up."

"You do make a persuasive argument." Alison rested her head on her pillow. "It'd be nice to simply relax and not worry about anything. This entire company could run without either of us for a long time."

"Exactly." He released her hand and lay on his side. "You know it, A. I shouldn't have to say it, but let's face it. There's always some crazy billionaire with a conspiracy or a group of vengeful dark wizards or aliens from a different dimension out there plotting to invade Earth."

Wow. When he says it like that, my life sounds crazy, but he also has a point.

"It's not your personal responsibility to run yourself into the ground because of the possibility that they might do something," he continued. "There are entire government agencies dedicated to protecting the country and the planet from threats. Seattle won't disappear simply because Alison Brownstone takes a few weeks to relax, exactly like LA didn't end because your dad semi-retired."

She closed her eyes while memories of all the threats Mason described flowed through her mind. "I know, I know. My dad now runs his restaurant and the occasional crap comes up that he has to deal with. Most of the time, his only real concern is keeping Mom happy and experimenting with meat and sauces. If he can do it, I can do it."

"Exactly. So let's do it. An off-grid vacation. Let's not even bring our phones."

Alison bolted up and her eyes snapped open. "Are you crazy? What if Drae makes a move?"

Mason laughed. "Let's say we go to one of these little kemana resorts. The worst-case scenario is Hana, Tahir, or Sonya hop on the train and head to a Starbucks that's probably—what, thirty minutes from us? An hour? And that's assuming they don't simply send us a message using magic. Tahir's an infomancer but he can still do all kinds of things without computers or phones. It's not 1722, A. So, what'll it be? Will you sit around worrying about some theoretical move that some princess might make six months from now, or will you live your life? Because right now, Drae's moved into your head and she hasn't even paid for the privilege."

"You're right." She nodded firmly. "I'll find us a pleasant off-the-grid vacation that's even better than the one we canceled. Screw Drae."

He grinned. "That's the spirit."

CHAPTER SEVEN

The Spider cruised down the road and Alison hummed under her breath. Mason sat beside her. Her trunk was full of their luggage, and her phone had been left at her house. The vacation had officially begun.

Nothing bad has happened. No Drae assassins showed up at my parents' place. Agent Latherby didn't call me at the last minute to request my help. I can do this. It'll be fun and relaxing, exactly like we planned.

"I almost can't believe it." Mason smiled.

"Can't believe what?" she asked.

"I was half-convinced you would find some new excuse for why we couldn't go on vacation," he explained. "Now, you're in a good mood, and we're on our way. Two weeks with no worries." He grinned. "After all that quality Alison time, I don't know if I'll be able to return to the real world."

She snorted. "I think you'll be sick of me. At least you can hide at work, but this will be concentrated Alison. Maybe you'll realize what married life will be like."

"I can never have enough of you, and I already know that marriage with you will be heaven."

Her cheeks heated. "I'm only saying we'll have considerable time on our hands."

"So?" he countered. "You chose a good place for it. A fancy resort in a New Hampshire kemana? That's inspired. If anything, I think it's even better than the island we planned to go to because it's a little more cut-off from the outside world."

"You have to thank Hana," she reminded him. "I wouldn't have even thought of the idea if she hadn't suggested it, and luck's finally smiling on me, too. I didn't tell you last night, but the place was booked up when I first called them. I tried a few others, and they were booked solid, too."

He nodded. "I'm not surprised. It's the middle of the summer. Did you pull the 'Do you know who I am?' card and get us a room?"

"Nope. I don't want to convince people ahead of time that I'm a pretentious bitch." She sucked in a breath and looked uncomfortable for a moment before her smile returned. "The first place called me back. They had some last-minute cancelations and I was willing to put down an immediate deposit." Her hands tightened around the wheel, and she took a few deep breaths. "A couple of weeks of relaxation with no Drow and no Tapestry. It'll be great. I only need to get there and stop worrying about Sonya, the company, Thomas, and everything."

Mason glanced at her with a playful, lop-sided smile. "It'll be fine, A. Sonya will be fine with Hana and Tahir. Ava will make sure everything stays on track at the company, and Jerry basically does his own thing most of the time anyway. The company will be there when we get back, and your parents don't need your help."

"I'll admit I'm still not sure about this whole privacy magic situation at the resort."

He laughed. "You've complained to Hana and me about people harassing you when you're on vacation and now, you don't like that they've set it up to avoid that situation? Don't go looking for trouble, A."

"I'm only saying that phones basically don't work in the kemana."

"Then it's a good thing we didn't bring them." His smile didn't dim in the slightest.

"But it's not only that," she persisted. "The heavy warding makes it difficult to even get general magical communication in and out. We might not be on an island in the middle of nowhere, but we'll effectively be that way in terms of communications."

"True, but that's half the point. We're going to relax, not read the news and messages. I read the stuff online, A. There are extensive grounds but they keep a close eye on who comes in and out of the resort itself. They have the situation under control enough that the government lets them keep more magical creatures than normal with fewer restrictions. You're making all this sound like a bad thing, but it's basically a place where you can relax without worrying that Drow troublemakers might arrive and stir up trouble." He laughed. "Seattle was here before you were even born, and it'll be here after we get back. Let's enjoy ourselves."

What am I doing? I was all ready to go and now, I'm worrying again.

"Assuming the Fremont Troll doesn't wake up," she mumbled.

"You need to stop being a control freak. I understand that you've inherited some of your Dad's OCD nature—or learned it since it wasn't transferred by DNA—but at least he channels it mostly into barbecue. I thought you might do that with cooking, but it's still only a hobby to you, not an obsession. I'm not complaining as such, but it would be nice if you could get out of your own way."

"I'm not a control freak," she replied. "I'm merely proactive in analyzing and exterminating potential annoyances."

Mason chuckled. "Whatever you say, A. Whatever you say. But please, promise me one thing."

"What?"

"You'll at least try to relax. I worry about you."

She kept one hand on the wheel as she raised the other to make her oath. "I promise to try to relax if the universe lets me."

An hour later, her Fiat was parked in an underground lot and her bags spirited away by black-clad employees of the Pacific Specialty Tours agency. They assured her that her luggage would be in her room once she arrived. She managed to convince them that she needed to keep one bag with a few toiletries, just in case. There were some things she really didn't want to have to conjure with magic.

A swirling opaque portal hung before the couple. It

floated below silver arches inscribed with arcane glyphs, a movable but permanent gateway.

Huh. If I can't master portals anytime soon, maybe I could try something like this? Maybe not. It's not like we can carry one around anywhere.

"Whatever work thing you're thinking about, stop," Mason suggested.

She nodded quickly. "You're right. I can do this. It starts here—the beginning of our big vacation. I've taken time off before. This is no different."

He laughed. "You sound like you're going to war, A. Come on. It'll be fun. This sounds like the perfect place, and given how much we're paying, I think they'll do their best to keep us relaxed and happy. We simply need to go in there with the right attitude."

"This is the big practice." She took a deep breath and released it slowly. "I'm doing this to convince myself we can do a full month for the honeymoon." She caught his hand with her free hand. "Let's do it."

It's a vacation. This isn't a raid on a dark wizard family headquarters or us fighting some deadly conspiracy group. It's merely my fiancé and I having a relaxing time at a resort. Screw Drae. She probably can't even afford a room here.

They stepped through the portal and emerged into a massive, vaulted grand lobby. Arched hallways led off in three directions and light flute music played in the background. A burbling marble fountain stood in one corner. The water erupted from sixteen different jets and curved in intricate and overlapping patterns possible only with magic. Light orbs floated above to provide warm lighting. Small trees grew in large clay pots, some well-manicured and normal green species and the others a rainbow of different colors.

In one corner of the room, a small humanoid shape made of fire danced in the air, its movement an aerial ballet. In another, large polished stones stacked themselves into elaborate structures before they spiraled away and settled to repeat the process. A light dust of different colors swirled in writhing columns in another corner.

"They have a little theme going," Alison observed as she took time to absorb it all. Magic radiated from everywhere in the room. It'd been a long time since she'd felt such a high level of background magic.

In the corner, a few wide-eyed people whispered amongst themselves while they pointed at the fountain, the light orbs, and some of the shifting paintings on the wall.

They did say you didn't have to be a magical to come here. I don't see any wands in that group.

Guests of various species lingered in the lobby and chatted quietly. Besides the obvious Oricerans such as elves and gnomes, more than a few witches and wizards walked through or stood in the lobby, their wands hanging openly from their belts. No one spared the couple more than a brief glance. A smiling dark-haired woman with solid black eyes stood behind a circular quartz counter in the middle of the lobby.

Alison looked behind her at the four wooden doors to the main entrance. There was no sign of the portal. "You must have to specifically ask for it to be opened."

"Probably," Mason replied. "Are you already looking to escape?"

"I was simply curious." Alison continued to study the

area. "But this place is probably so warded I wonder if you can open a direct portal here without real difficulty."

A rather overweight pixie fluttered past her in the company of a gnome in a trilby. "This place is nice," the pixie announced, her voice deep and rough as if she'd inhaled an entire warehouse of cigarettes in a day.

"I thought you would like it, Madge," the gnome replied and adjusted his hat.

"I'm kind of reminded of the School of Necessary Magic." Alison released the breath she didn't even know she'd been holding.

Mason snickered. "I didn't realize it was that fancy."

"I used to think it was only because it was magical, but no, it was fancy." She smiled. "I can relax here."

CHAPTER EIGHT

"I'll take your bag, ma'am," a woman said cheerfully behind them. The couple had finished check-in at the quartz desk and turned at the sound of the voice.

A smiling Nicht bellhop in a black-and-white uniform stood there, her arm outstretched and her leathery wings folded behind her back.

While Alison didn't really need someone to carry a single bag, she'd already paid a full-service baggage-handling fee, so there was no reason not to let the smiling woman do her job. She handed the bag over and the bellhop took it.

"Follow me, sir, ma'am," she requested and turned toward one of the hallways. "I'll show you to your room."

I feel kind of weird about this level of service, but it's not like I've never stayed in a nice place before. I merely need to ease into it.

They trailed after her.

"This place must really be coming up in the world," the bellhop commented.

"Oh?" she asked. "Why do you say that?"

The woman nodded. "There are many high-quality guests who stay with us, but you're one of our more famous ones. I would love it if your father did, but from what I've read, this isn't his kind of place."

"You could say that." She sighed. "The clerk knew who I was, but I hoped that was only because she handled the reservations. You recognized me, too?"

"Of course, Miss Brownstone." The Nicht smiled. "Don't worry, though. We strive to keep your stay comfortable and private. We won't allow any other guests to bother you in any way. If you have any concerns, let staff know and we'll deal with it immediately."

"I'm not that worried. I'm only hoping I can relax."

Did I let the lack of reaction in the lobby trick me? Maybe not. She's nice and chatty but it's not like she's asked for an autograph.

"What do you mean by coming up in the world?" Mason asked.

They entered the hall where more moving magical paintings decorated the walls. Unlike the nature scenes that defined the lobby, the new paintings were scenes depicting minor historical figures from local kemana history, such as a witch who stopped a magical plague in a surface village in the seventeenth century, only to be hung when a man saw her in the forest with her wand.

The bellhop slowed and turned to whisper. "I probably shouldn't say this. Management hates it if we break the spell of luxury, but the truth is that this kemana was dying a few years back. Everyone younger was moving out, then they built this place and it gave many of us a reason to stay.

My family's lived here for several generations and I didn't want to leave, but it was becoming a ghost town and there are so many more opportunities for magicals than there were when we were kids." She sighed. "I understand why people don't want to live in a kemana in a world where magic's no longer restricted or secret, but I really didn't want to leave the place I grew up in." She gasped and put a hand to her face as her pale cheeks reddened. "I'm sorry. That was inappropriate. I shouldn't have said any of that. I don't even know why I did. It's simply that I felt like I could talk to you that way. It was presumptuous. I'm sorry if I made you uncomfortable, Miss Brownstone."

Alison shook her head and offered her a gentle smile. "It's okay. You can call me Alison. I'm here because I wanted a pleasant place where people wouldn't gawk at me."

The bellhop nodded at her wings. "That's the other thing. It's not always the case that my wings don't come out when I'm away from the kemana. When I was young, they told me it wouldn't be in my lifetime that my wings would come out without the kemana, but it hasn't worked out that way. There's more magic in many more cities than they said there would be."

"I think the gates haven't been open at all in thousands of years, and people don't always know how things will work out," she suggested. "Trust me. In my line of work, I've run into any number of surprises, so I don't assume anything about how magic will work anymore."

"That's the best attitude." Their guide continued down the hallway, a smile on her face. She stopped in front of a silver platform nestled in a small alcove. Four sapphires were inset, one in each of the corners. She gestured to the platform and they stepped on before she joined them.

Alison looked up. A bright shaft extended several floors above them. It was a magical elevator.

Some of the displays in the resort came off as a little excessive to her, but if they were charged top dollar to also draw rich non-magicals, it didn't hurt to give them a taste of a world where magic was freer.

"Room 4432," the bellhop requested.

Blue walls of light appeared around the platform and it ascended at a comfortable speed. It passed an entrance to a hallway on the second floor and third floor before it stopped on the fourth floor. The wall vanished on one side to provide access into the hallway.

Nice, fool-proof spells. This whole place is the kind of thing someone from the Entrepreneur's Club at my school might have come up with.

The bellhop stepped off the elevator and gestured grandly into the corridor. "Your room is down here. The room's wards should already be keyed to you. If you need anything, you can ring the bell in your room and a staffer will be there shortly."

The couple stepped off the elevator and followed the Nicht down the lushly carpeted hallway. Unlike the first floor, elaborate vases on stands provided the decoration. The soft floral scent permeating the air relaxed Alison, but there was no obvious source—more magic for the sake of magic, she realized.

They continued until they arrived at their room.

"Open room 4432," the bellhop ordered.

The door unlocked itself and swung open. She stepped

inside and set Alison's bag atop the mattress of the huge four-poster bed. Despite all the magic, the room itself looked like a spacious but normal hotel room, although there was a noticeable lack of a television or phone. A brass bell stood on one of the nightstands. Huge curtains blocked the view of their balcony.

"Thank you," Alison said after she and Mason entered.

The woman smiled and stepped outside. Instantly, the door closed behind her.

"I'm glad they have that service fee," she commented. "I didn't even think about bringing cash."

"The result of an increasingly cashless society, even if this place isn't plugged into the Internet."

Alison meandered to the curtains and pulled them open. A large balcony extended beyond double glass doors and overlooked a sprawling, tiered, and colorful multi-acre garden. Vibrant flowers and blooming shrubs planted in careful patterns around almost mazelike walkways composed much of it, but huge trees extended hundreds of feet into the air and were surrounded by copses of smaller trees softened by groupings of flowers. A faint, dull blue glow reflected from the roof of the kemana itself, but much of it was washed out by the bright light from the light orbs and light poles of the resort and the town around it.

A soft gasp escaped her. "That's very beautiful. I wonder if druids or Wood Elves maintain it."

"Maybe." Mason surveyed the garden. "At least it's not a hedge maze."

"I could always fly over it." She grinned and closed the curtains. The beautiful view aside, she wanted privacy for her first day at the resort.

He sat on the edge of the bed. "I always feel weird coming to a kemana."

"Why is that?" She settled beside him.

"Because I've spent most of my life in a city without one. Living and working in Seattle means not having to step into them all that often." He shook his head. "And I'm too young to really remember a time where a separate magical town made as much sense. I'm honestly surprised that governments allow them, even if they've progressed and established more authority than what existed back in the day. It's like having entire separate city-states living beneath you. Sometimes, I'm amazed there hasn't been a mundane-magical war."

She wrinkled her nose. "We've been lucky. If we hadn't stopped Scott Carlyle, there very well might have been."

"Well, he's locked up now where he hopefully can't stir up more trouble." He looked thoughtful. "But it's weird how these places are still around. What that Nicht says makes some sense, but there are certain political realities to these places even existing."

"I don't know. If you think about it, the gates only began opening a few decades ago and they were closed for thousands of years. If anything, I'm surprised by how quickly things have changed." She patted his shoulder. "We've gone from almost everyone believing magic was something silly people believed in the past to magical criminals and technomagic companies. They've even used magic to work on that moon base. The world of adult Thomas might be totally different than what we're used to."

Mason considered that for a moment before he nodded

slightly, although he remained thoughtful. "Sure. When you put it that way, it all makes sense. I guess it's easy to get too comfortable and familiar with how things are. Comfortable isn't always the same thing as the best, though."

"I had some interesting times in the kemana near the School of Necessary Magic," she pointed out. "But I know what you mean. I spent so many years without knowing I had true magic so I suppose I'll always be more of a surface girl in my heart."

He shrugged. "I was raised in a magical family and I'm that way. I think most people craved something more normal than hiding from billions of others. Places like this are a great place to spend a few weeks, but Earth can't move forward if the magicals and non-magicals don't mix."

"But I can feel the higher level of magic here, too." She raised her hand and shadow tendrils extended from her palm.

"Is that some big spell you're planning to do?"

"No, but there are a few things I might want to try while I'm here. Things I have more trouble accomplishing outside a kemana."

Mason frowned. "That's fine, A, but remember that we're here to relax, not practice techniques."

"Sure, I know that." Alison poked her tongue out of the corner of her mouth and furrowed her brow in concentration. The shadow tendrils formed into a small copy of her. "But it's not like I'll sleep and eat the entire time."

His gaze shifted to her bag where his wand was stored, but he didn't retrieve it. Instead, he leaned over and took a pamphlet from the nightstand. "All these over-the-top spells and they have a plain old brochure in the end." He chuckled. "Paper's not magic, but maybe they have some enchanted printing press or something they used."

She dissipated the tendrils, fell back on the bed, and spread her arms wide. "Okay, I'm here. Now what? You don't want me to worry about practicing magic, so let's get going on our first day of off-the-grid vacation."

"There was a long list of things to do on that website," he replied. He thumbed through the brochure. "They list many of them here, too. Apparently, they've created different environments, not only things like that garden. They even have an arena where people can fight fake monsters."

Her eyes gleamed and she sat up. "Let's do that, then."

He set the brochure down and fixed her with an exasperated look. "So, we're on vacation and you're supposed to relax, and you basically want to do the purely magical version of our tac room?"

"Why not?" She shrugged. "There's nothing that says you can't exercise while on vacation, right?"

"Oh, A, I'll get you to relax if it kills me."

CHAPTER NINE

A few minutes later, after changing into sweatpants and tennis shoes, the couple left their room and took the elevator to the first floor. The blue safety wall dropped but they couldn't exit. A smiling young brown-haired woman stood there in a floral print sundress, her hands clasped together and pure euphoria on her face as she stared directly ahead.

Okay. That's...different.

Several seconds passed, but the woman didn't move. She turned her head slowly from side to side and murmured quietly to herself. "Elevator...glass...magic," was all Alison could make out.

She stared expectantly at the stranger before she finally cleared her throat. "Is something wrong? Do you need help?"

The lithe woman blinked and stepped back and a splash of pink appeared on her cheeks. "Oh, I'm sorry. I've gone up and down several times. And I know it's not that different than a normal elevator, but I can't get over it. The concept is so cool. Magic elevator."

"Oh, it is that." She glanced at the platform. In a sense, the elevator might be flashy but it paled in comparison to magic such as portals or even the Starbucks' train. She always assumed most people would be far more impressed by magic that accomplished something technology couldn't easily replicate.

The woman's blush deepened and she looked away. "I'm so excited to be here. Everything's so different and new. It's like I'm Charlie and it's all too much for me to not stand here and drool. I keep expecting someone to pinch me and I'll wake up and realize I'm back working swing shift at home."

They stepped off the elevator and exchanged looks. The woman seemed harmless, if overly excitable.

"Charlie?" Alison asked. "Who's Charlie?"

"Charlie. Like, you know, *Charlie and the Chocolate Factory.*" The woman shrugged. "I love that book. I've seen all the movie versions too. I think the 2034 version is the best, though. What they did with the Oompa Loompas was great. I know all those gnomes picketed the movie, but they didn't say the Oompa Loompas were gnomes. They merely happen to resemble gnomes."

"Oh. Yeah, I've seen that one. I haven't read the book, though." Alison remained convinced that Roald Dahl was a secret magical given the flavor of the magical strangeness in his books. There were more than a few magical authors who had passed off thinly disguised anecdotes from their lives as fiction before the truth of Oriceran came out, but she'd never been able to confirm that Dahl was anything other than a creative Englishman. Perhaps that was his final magic trick on both worlds.

Mason scrutinized the woman before he held his wand up. "I apologize if I'm assuming too much, but you're not a magical, are you?"

"Me? Magical?" The woman uttered a merry titter. "I wish." She shook her head and extended a hand.

He gave it a light shake and Alison did as well.

"Anyway, I'm Jade the non-magical. I'm merely a normal, not-weird plain human." She grimaced. "Not to say that magicals are weird, but I have no special powers with or without a wand. I can't change into an animal or fly. I'm nothing more than a girl from a small town in Nebraska. Go Huskers." She laughed. "We don't have any magicals in my town either. I did see Nadina once when she visited a barbecue place in Omaha, though. She is so beautiful and so nice, and her barbecue is ridiculously good."

"I've had it," Alison replied with a smile.

Jade smiled at her. "You probably get this a lot and I'm sorry if I sound like a total fangirl or something, but you look so much like Alison Brownstone."

She chuckled and shrugged. "Maybe I shouldn't admit this, but I am Alison Brownstone."

The woman gasped. "Wow! I really am lucky." She clapped gleefully. "They said I might run into celebrities here, but I thought they meant boring celebrities. You know, like actors or musicians or politicians, not someone like you. I think I saw a congressman earlier, but I'm not sure. I don't pay that much attention to that kind of thing, and half of them kind of look the same to me because every time you see them, they're in suits."

"I can understand that." She managed an easy smile. "You mentioned feeling like Charlie. If you're like Charlie, does that mean you won a contest? This might not be a magical chocolate factory that no one has visited before, but at least it's magical and has a few gnomes."

She didn't intend the question to sound rude, but everything about Jade—from her dress to demeanor—suggested a woman born far from privilege, wealth, or magic and who had never seen magicals offline before. Her school experience and current residence in the techno-magic capital of the US could sometimes blind Alison to exactly how many people never ran into magicals in their day-to-day lives. The gates might be open, but Earth wasn't Oriceran. For billions of people, magicals were only people they read about or saw on the news.

Jade nodded quickly, her bright smile infectious. "I listen to the *All Things Oriceran* podcast. I'm, like, their biggest fan. I've listened to every episode, sometimes more than once." She took a few quick breaths. "Sorry, I'm getting off-track. Anyway, they had a contest on the Fourth of July for their one-hundredth episode. I've never won anything before in my life, let alone an all-expenses-paid two-week vacation to a luxury resort. Even if it wasn't a magical place, it'd be ridiculously good luck." She uttered a squeaky giggle. "And I'm so excited to meet you, but I get it. You're on vacation, too. I won't bother you about auto-graphs or cool things you and your dad have done. I only want you to know that I'm a big fan—strong woman role model and all that."

I don't know if I count since I was born with strong magic, but I don't want to burst her bubble. It's great to see someone not loaded down with cynicism for a change. Even Hana, as bubbly as she is, has that dark core.

"I appreciate it," she responded. "It sounds like you're really enjoying your trip so far."

"Oh, so much. I only got here today."

"Are you here with anyone?"

Jade shook her head and smiled at Mason. "Not all of us are blessed with hot wizard boyfriends."

He grinned. "No, not everyone is."

Alison rolled her eyes. "Don't feed his ego too much, but he's a good guy."

The woman pointed at the lobby. "I wonder if the entire world will be like this place once the gates are fully open. I know I'll be long dead, but it's funny to think about a magical world of wonder. The entire Earth as the chocolate factory with way less Oompa Loompas."

For a moment, Alison worried she would need to find a way to bring the encounter to an end without seeming too rude, but the experience wasn't awful. Chatting with an excited guest wasn't the same thing as being hounded by the media, let alone assassins, criminals, or even the occasional courier in need of Drow princess muscle. The woman's reaction to everything in the hotel reminded her of her initial feelings when she arrived at the School of Necessary Magic.

Wonder wasn't an awful thing. Magic might be a tool but it was still magic. Sometimes, she felt twice her age, her experiences having tested her soul since the betrayal by her biological father.

With all my power and ability, I can't turn the clock back. There's no point in even worrying about it. At least everything left from my school days has been handled.

"Maybe Earth will end up like that," she conceded and pulled herself from her introspection. "Maybe not. There are interesting and awe-inspiring places on Oriceran, but many places are surprisingly mundane by Earth standards. Magic's much like technology and sometimes, like you shouldn't use a complicated gadget to do something simple, you shouldn't use a complicated spell for something you could do without difficulty or magic. This place sets out to be impressive, so they use considerable magic in ways that aren't all that efficient. At my company, I use more magic than many others, but I don't use most of what they use here."

Jade considered the response and finally nodded. "That makes sense now that you explain it that way. This is a luxury resort. It'd be like me going to a non-magical resort and thinking every building in the country is like that."

"Exactly."

"Everything in the chocolate factory didn't always have a point, but I suppose real-life can't be like a book or a movie." She sighed. "It makes me think. If only we could combine the best of technology and magic." She stared at the floor and fiddled with the hem of her dress. "That's why what happened with Scott Carlyle is so sad. The other rich guy, too, but he seemed like he didn't push things as much. At least that's what all the articles said."

Alison's jaw tightened. "Scott Carlyle? You think what happened to him was sad?"

She can't be anti-magical and then be happy to be in a place like this. What gives?

The woman looked up and swallowed with an apologetic expression. "I'm not saying it's bad he went to jail. What he did was unforgivable. It was terrorism. The government even said so. It's only that I used to be a big fan before I found out he was..." She sighed. "That he was evil. I thought he would help to revolutionize the world with technomagic and then he... Well, you know what he did better than anyone. I'm sorry you had to go through all that."

"Yes, I do," she muttered. "And thanks." She tried to keep the venom out of her voice but failed.

You always find a way to weasel back, don't you, Scott? Can't you simply be a good boy and rot in prison until everyone forgets you even existed?

Mason stepped forward and squeezed her hand. "Technomagic research doesn't stop simply because Carlyle went to jail, Jade. He was only one man, and I know his company's been disrupted, but the advances will continue with time and effort."

Jade shook her head. "Lost opportunities and lost momentum. I read about it in an article. Now that I'm here, I can't help but think about what we could have if he had stayed a good guy." Her breath caught. "Uh...well, I should let you go. I'm sure you have better things to do on vacation than talk with a random woman who works at a convenience store." She rushed onto the elevator, her face red. "Fifth floor, please."

The blue wall appeared and the elevator rose. The

woman avoided looking directly at them as it carried her to the upper floors.

Alison groaned. "That was fun for the first half of that conversation at least."

He squeezed her hand again. "Don't hold it against her. Too many people were fooled by him, A. She's merely a little overwhelmed to be here and she probably didn't even think about what she was saying until it came out of her mouth."

"I'm not mad at her. I know people were fooled. That list includes me, after all. The asshole sat there and controlled me like a puppet after he'd poisoned me with his disease. I simply didn't expect to hear his name on vacation. It wasn't the best way to start things out." She frowned. "Damn it."

Mason nodded toward the lobby. "Forget Carlyle. He's rotting in jail and you're at a resort. The best way to get your revenge is to have a good time while he thinks about how salty his prison food is and how he'll never be free. Even all those terrorists dedicated to helping him are gone."

"You're right." She took a few deep, cleansing breaths. Of course Jade would comment on the incident. If it wasn't something like that, it would have been something involving someone dangerous and ruthless—the Seventh Order and Vancouver or the Fremont Troll or one of countless bounties. Her career highlights usually included something that involved violence as well as someone who had caused suffering. The two seemed to go hand in hand.

I should be used to it by now, or maybe it's a good thing that I don't get used to it so I always realize the kind of life I lead and all the implications. Dad and Mom had to settle down eventually. Maybe I will sooner rather than later.

Look out, Mason. You have me on vacation, which means I have that much more time to brood and think.

The couple continued down the hallway. Alison did her best to not Brownstone Brood but failed. She spared a look behind her and regret clawed at her mind. It wasn't Jade's fault that Scott Carlyle turned out to be a sociopathic scheming asshole. It wasn't anyone's but his. Many people had followed him and most of them had already paid, but he was the one who used his charisma and resources for a dark cause instead of improving the world.

A white-haired young woman now stood near the elevators in the distance. She was too far away for Alison to discern her features, but her build and even her jeans and red jacket invoked someone all too familiar.

"What the—" She stopped and stared. "It can't be."

Her doppelganger stepped onto the elevator. A blue light wall appeared, and the woman headed to the second floor and disappeared from sight.

Mason continued for a few feet before he stopped and turned. "What's wrong?"

"There's a woman who looks like me," she explained.

He looked down the hallway. "I don't see anyone."

"She got on the elevator. Okay, I didn't get a good look at her face, but she had white hair and similar taste in clothes." She had even brought a red denim coat even if she wasn't wearing it at the moment.

"Are you saying I can have two Alisons on vacation?"

He grinned and waggled his eyebrows. "Jade's right. This truly is a place of wonder and grand imagination."

"Don't make me hurt you." She rolled her eyes as they entered the lobby.

"You're not the only young woman on the planet with white hair, you know, let alone on Oriceran. And I know you don't care much about fashion, but you're not exactly unique in your tastes, A."

"Sure, it's only—"

"Alison?" interrupted a surprise-filled voice from behind them. "It can't be."

She turned toward the new arrival and gaped. It was another familiar face.

"Okay, Mason, are you now going to tell me Izzie isn't standing right in front of me?"

Izzie stared at her with her mouth parted in slight surprise. Given the elaborate updo, body-hugging black dress, and high heels, she wasn't there on a bounty hunt unless it involved infiltrating a high-class ball.

He laughed. "No, that's her. Nice to see you again, Izzie." He extended a hand and she shook it.

"Hey, Alison." Her friend chuckled. "This is about the last place I expected to run into you. Okay, maybe not the last place. Some kind of New Veil rally might be the last place, but this at least makes the list of highly improbable places to meet Alison Brownstone."

"Same. What are you doing here?" She made a show of studying her. "Classy, by the way. I like it."

Izzie rubbed the back of her neck and her cheeks colored slightly. "I had to go back to my room to get something quickly. I left Luke waiting. We're having a little drink in one of the fancier resort restaurants. I wanted something simpler, but he insisted he wanted to see me all dressed up and...uh...you know how guys can be. And when a wolf sets his mind on something, it's sometimes better to simply roll with it."

Mason smirked. "Yes, men can be stubborn, wolves or otherwise."

"You're here with Luke?" Alison grinned. "That makes sense. A romantic getaway? Things really have progressed, huh?"

The other woman rolled her eyes. "It's not a big deal and he's paying, so what was I going to do, tell him no? But forget about that. You and Mason are here. We should have lunch or dinner together." She leaned forward to look past them. "I assume you didn't bring the whole crew?"

"Nope. It's only Mason and me. Hana and the others are holding the fort down in Seattle."

He nodded his agreement. "We should get together. I like the idea. Good friends and good wine."

"We're in Room 3211."

"Room 4432," Alison replied. "You get what you need and have your drink with Luke. We'll catch up with you. We were going to try their little arena. It was merely for a little exercise at first, but I need to burn some frustration off."

Izzie's eyes lit up. "You know, relaxing is fun, but a little exercise doesn't hurt." She looked at her dress. "I'll go get Luke. We can change and join you if you don't mind waiting. I think it'd be fun for all four of us to kick ass together."

"I don't mind, but..." She waved her hands in front of

her chest. "You don't have to. I don't want to mess your fancy date up."

Her friend shook her head. "The chances of us running into each other like this are exceptionally low, especially when we're relaxing and don't have anything hanging over our heads. I think we should take advantage of it. Luke and I are together, but he's your friend, too. It's like this is a sign or something." She looked at Mason. "If that's okay with you? I don't want to mess up any plans you two had. Maybe you really wanted only Alison and you ass-kicking time together."

"No, I'd love it if you two could join us." He smiled. "I don't have any deep expectations for this trip. I don't care as long these two weeks end with Alison more relaxed than before we arrived."

"Then it's a double-date for the arena. I'll be right back. Luke will be so surprised." She pivoted on her heel and rushed toward the opposite hall, her agility surprising giving the stilts disguised as shoes on her feet. She skirted two gnomes and a scowling Light Elf in a brown robe.

"Izzie and Luke, huh?" Alison murmured. "This is practically a School of Necessary Magic reunion." A cold chill passed over her, and she shivered. She turned her head slowly.

"A, what's wrong?" Mason asked.

"It felt like someone was watching me."

No one paid any obvious attention to her in the lobby. Only a few employees walked down the hall carrying a few boxes on floating trays.

She swept her gaze around the area but found nothing odd, only the expected gratuitous magical displays. There were no doppelgangers or suspicious men and no shimmer in the air that might betray a hidden magical.

He patted her shoulder. "Let's have fun with your friends. All right?"

"Sure," she murmured but the sensation of being watched remained. "I need to focus only on fun."

CHAPTER TEN

It didn't take long for Izzie to return with Luke in tow. After a quick exchange of greetings, they hurried to their room to change before rendezvousing again with Alison and Mason in the lobby. The earlier sensation of being watched faded with Luke's arrival and allowed her to focus on the anticipation of spending time with her old friends and not on her paranoia.

The two couples traversed the maze of hallways with the help of a few careful questions asked of the occasional employee until they arrived at the far side of the resort. A small line had formed in front of two large doors with the words *SAPPHIRE SPRING RESORT RECREATIONAL ARENA* in glowing letters above.

Maybe it is weird to want to do this kind of thing on vacation but returning to the familiar is a good way to relax. If I keep telling myself that, I might even start to believe it.

Two uniformed Kilomea stood behind a large counter along the wall and their uniforms strained at the seams. They allowed parties to enter for fifteen- to twenty-minute sessions. Mason had already checked in with them and chosen a scenario before he rejoined the other three at the end of the line.

Luke took the opportunity to crouch and stretch once he'd filled out his decidedly non-magical safety waiver forms. "I still can't believe we ran into you two here. Good timing for once."

Izzie elbowed him. "What's that supposed to mean?"

"Until recently, every time one of us got together with Alison, it generally involved a huge battle and significant property damage." He grinned.

She shrugged. "I'll give you that."

"Thanks." Alison laughed.

"I'm not saying it's your fault, but you can't deny it."

Mason smiled. "That does tend to happen around her, regardless of whether she's with her old school friends or not."

The shifter completed his stretch and stood. "Forget all that. I'm simply happy we found each other. Maybe somewhere, Mara's casting a reunion spell. We can get the entire gang back together."

"That's more trouble than we all need." His girlfriend laughed.

Alison shrugged and kept a smile on her face despite the paranoia that threatened to resurface. She was glad to see her friends, but now that Luke mentioned the fortuitous nature of their meeting, she couldn't help but think running into them so unexpectedly might be a plot. The harder she pushed the thought down, the stronger it returned.

Is it because that woman mentioned Scott Carlyle? Am I that wound up? It's not like Izzie and Luke can be shoved around like chess pieces. She outran the Seventh Order for years and knows how to take care of herself. Luke's fought hard to get where he is and he's surrounded by scheming politicians all the time.

Mason twirled his wand in his fingers. "I notice you're looking forward to this arena, Luke."

The other man laughed. "You're damned right I am. I know every second of every day in Congress that people think of me as a shifter first and a congressman second, and I have to act accordingly. I think many people expect me to change into a wolf and eat someone on the floor at any time. I've done my best to demystify things, but old beliefs die hard and I know that every time I shift or do anything the average voter thinks is unusual, I place myself at risk. I can't wait to cut loose a little where there are no reporters around to accuse me of becoming a dangerous brutal beast that's out of control."

"I hadn't thought about it that way," the life wizard admitted.

"Yet another reason I don't ever want to become a politician," Alison interjected. "It's bad enough how much people watch me now. I can only imagine a Brownstone trying to enter politics. It'd be a freaking train wreck."

"I'd vote for you." Mason winked.

"I bet you would." She turned to Izzie. "Have you guys been here a while?"

Her friend shook her head. "Nope, only since yesterday. We've talked about a real getaway for the two of us, but Congress had their early recess this year, so it seemed like a perfect time. It kind of came up in conversation a couple of weeks ago and we decided to take the plunge."

"How did you hear about this place?"

"I was the one who suggested it," Luke explained. "They've actually tried to get me to come here for a while and even offered me a stay for free. I turned that part down to avoid an appearance of impropriety, but I did want to have a look because of their reputation for catering to magicals. Spending time with the pack is all well and good, but I know that might get boring for Izzie, and I wanted an environment where there were no expectations for either of us."

"I never said the pack was boring," she complained.

He grinned. "I didn't say you did, but that doesn't make it any less true because of where we all ended up after I went to school. They know my situation. I'm a politician now, so I don't spend as much time with them and they understand that, but it also means things can settle into certain old patterns when I do return. Boring patterns for you."

She muttered under her breath.

One of the Kilomea opened the door and a sweating trio of witches in spandex emerged, all laughing and gesturing with their wands. A jagged tear in one woman's outfit suggested something large had clawed one of them, but there was no wound which suggested healing magic or a potion, most likely.

They weren't kidding in their safety waivers.

"I thought that dragon had you," one of the witches exclaimed. "Munch, munch, bitch!"

"As if," the other responded and rolled her eyes. "I've fought real dragons bigger than that."

"Are you high on Dust now? 'Cause I don't believe that for a second."

"I dated a dragon once," the third woman stated.

The other two laughed. "Bullshit."

"Next group," the other Kilomea bellowed.

The witches winced and hurried away. The six guests at the head of the line shuffled inside before the staffers slammed the door behind them and scowled. Alison couldn't tell if they always looked like that or if they merely hated their jobs.

Izzie smiled at her. "Congratulations again on the new brother, by the way. I thought about visiting after your call, but I kind of got the feeling the last thing your parents needed was more people hanging around with his surprise arrival and all, let alone everything else that happened."

"Yeah, they've kept it low-key," she responded. "A few visitors. There was no way they could keep Trey from seeing the littlest Brownstone, but it was a tight circle those few first weeks." She gestured to Izzie and Luke. "But this worked out well with us getting to see each other so soon. Thomas is cute, but he's still a newborn. He doesn't do much but eat, sleep, and poop."

She tried to push them down, but dark thoughts again floated to the surface.

The timing is very strange. If this place has tried to get Luke to come for a while, they might have made a recent attempt to push him over the line. But from what Izzie said, it doesn't seem like they were manipulated into coming here after I called. But maybe I was somehow pushed toward them? Could someone have hacked Hana's phone to send an ad?

Wait. That doesn't make sense. There's no way that would happen without Tahir knowing.

There was a fine line between prudent caution and raging paranoia, and she wasn't so sure she hadn't flown over it with a rocket strapped to her back.

Mason sighed. "What's going on, A?"

She startled and looked at him. "What do you mean? Nothing. I'm simply waiting." It wasn't technically a lie.

"No, there's definitely something going on. I know that look." He scrunched his face and narrowed his eyes in imitation of her in deep thought. "This is Alison Brownstone deeply pondering something and not relaxing. Brooding and pondering you can do any other time, not when we're here. We're on vacation. So, spill. What has you spun up?"

Izzie and Luke turned their curious gazes on her.

"It's nothing. I simply have difficulty turning my mind off, maybe because of what that woman said. It started me thinking about things. It's not a big deal."

He pinched the bridge of his nose. "A, it's the first day. You have to try."

"What woman?" her friend asked with a frown. "Don't tell me someone harassed you here of all places? If they did, tell the staff. They'll kick them out immediately, especially someone who is annoying someone as famous as you. The management would probably piss themselves if they thought Alison Brownstone would go around talking about how terrible her experience was at the resort. It's one of the reasons they've bent over backward for Luke, too."

"It's not like that." She gestured toward the other end of

the hallway. "We ran into a non-magical woman who won a contest to come here. She's excited to be around so much magic and magicals. It was kind of cute in a way. Toward the end of the conversation, though, she happened to mention Scott Carlyle."

Izzie grimaced. "Ouch. Yeah, I can see how that might ruin your mood."

Luke uttered a low growl and his eyes flashed yellow. "The last I heard, he's still rotting in prison. He'll die in prison, the bastard."

"He's still there," she confirmed. "I think I'm merely in a suspicious mood now because once he was mentioned, I can't help but remember what happened with him and how he manipulated me."

The other woman's breath caught. "Oh, I get it." She nodded. "I totally get it. Everything makes perfect sense now."

The shifter frowned. "I don't get it. What makes perfect sense?"

"This is a rabbit hole you might not want to go down," Mason warned.

"Alison's thinking there's some conspiracy that pushed us together because of how we happened to run into each other." Izzie gestured broadly with her arms. "And she's probably trying to figure out if the conspiracy is targeting you, me, her, or all of us." She looked at Mason. "They're probably not trying to kill you. It's simply less likely, all things considered. No offense."

He laughed. "None taken. Dealing with Alison's enemies is enough. I don't need my own. I'm an ex-body-guard, anyway. I'm supposed to guard the target, not be the target."

Luke shook his head. "It's merely a coincidence. I didn't receive any special messages, calls, or offers recently, and the Secret Service, FBI, and PDA have all checked this place out previously. It's totally on the up and up."

The faces of the two Kilomea twitched.

Yeah, this is probably a little insulting from their perspective. It's hard to say, "It's not you. It's us. We tend to be a magnet for murderous magical conspiracies. Sorry!"

"I'm not saying this place is corrupt," she whispered. There was no reason to offend the staff on their first day. "I'm only saying we all have more than our fair share of enemies so it's good to be careful."

"I am careful," Luke replied. "I receive many threats. There are countless people out there who don't like the idea of a shifter in Congress, and not all of them are non-magicals. But let's be honest about this, Alison. The main threat that linked all three of us was the Seventh Order, and they've been annihilated. I'm not saying no one else would ever target me or Izzie, and I know you have problems, but I honestly think you're connecting dots that don't go together. Sometimes, a coincidence is merely a coincidence."

Mason snorted. "He's right, A. You shouldn't see an assassin in every shadow."

"Not any assassin. One particular assassin—or at least her lackeys." She took a deep breath. "What about Drae?"

"Drae?" Izzie frowned. "Isn't that one of the Drow princesses?"

She nodded. "Yes. She's a schemer. Maybe she's trying to target my friends."

"Or maybe it's simply a big coincidence." The shifter grinned. "Damn, Alison. I thought I needed a vacation, but you need to be stranded on a warded island for security contractor detox." He looked at Mason. "Is she always like this now? I thought it'd improve when the Seventh Order was destroyed. I know you all had other trouble, but Izzie told me that was taken care of."

"She's not like this all the time," the life wizard replied. "Only on days that end in Y. This is why I'm glad we came here—no phones and minimal contact with the outside world."

Alison's cheeks heated and she sighed. "Maybe you're right. I am seeing assassins in the shadows." She took a deep breath and released it slowly. "I'm sorry. I'll try to enjoy this place for what it is. It's hard to switch off, though."

Izzie gave her a sympathetic smile. "I know, Alison. Luke and I understand the kind of things you've been through. Let's simply have our little fight and pretend it's all Drow assassins and Seventh Order hitmen."

"We should have gone to hammocks on an island somewhere," Mason mumbled.

CHAPTER ELEVEN

The group stepped through the doors into a narrow, dark hallway lined with light-blue crystal. It continued for about twenty yards before it ended at another set of thick metal doors. The group stepped into the arena, and the doors slammed shut behind them.

"That's not ominous," Alison muttered.

Izzie grinned. "What's a fight without a little tension?"

Other than the circular nature of the room, calling it an arena was somewhat misleading. A bright false sky covered the roof above and the heat of the fake sun beat down on them. They stood at an intersection in what resembled a destroyed city block, complete with several worn brick buildings, alleys, and rusted cars. Three other distinct areas bordered the city block. One was a blasted desert land-scape filled with cacti and rocky bluffs and even a few stereotypical cattle skulls. Another zone was a dense jungle, and the last was a rocky beach beside the ocean. Magical energy choked the entire room and the walls and it was hard to distinguish what might be real and what was an illusion.

"I wonder why they don't use something like a Louper system," Izzie muttered.

"A game is simply a game," Mason replied. "It's also why at our office, we have an actual course. At the end of the day, even magical VR is still VR." He pointed to a nearby building covered in graffiti reading *DOWN WITH RHAZ-DON. UP WITH ORICERAN.* "This is more limited in some ways because they can't have so many varied environments at the touch of a button, but people feel the risk better."

"But this isn't a training room for security contractors," the woman countered. "It's merely somewhere for guests to blow off steam."

"What's more memorable—skydiving or VR skydiving?"

"Point taken."

"According to the brochure, they change the arena every few weeks, but the magic's extremely complicated." He pointed at the doors. "The fact that this is an artificial but not virtual environment is also why we didn't enter the room directly. From what I read, they have numerous defensive spells layered to protect the rest of the resort. That said, certain Brownstones and Berens should probably keep their magic in check." He smirked. "According to the release forms, we agreed to limit any use of ranged spells of 'significant destructive nature.' And I don't think even having a congressman with us would be enough to make up for it."

Luke snickered. "I'd like to avoid any negative media attention resulting from my vacation. It's amazing that I managed to duck out without any of those vultures realizing it and trying to find me."

Izzie offered him a salute. "Aye, aye, sir. No blowing up half the building."

"I'm not here to nuke the entire room." Alison looked from one to the other. "I'll stick to the basics. There's more than enough here to take advantage of the terrain. You never did tell me what scenario you chose." She mock-glared at Mason. "It had better not involve giant bugs. If it does, I'll have to reconsider blowing up half the building."

He shook his head. "I wanted something relaxing and mindless, so I found something silly and straightforward. There will be no giant bugs, no terrorists, no dark wizards, and nothing that'll put you in a bad mood."

"That all sounds good except for one part."

"What?"

"Silly. I don't know if I like the sound of that. Silly is subjective." She studied him with suspicion.

"I'm fairly sure you would prefer silly over grittier, more realistic stuff. Anyway, you'll see when things start. Since we're only here to cut loose, I asked them to send the opponents at us rather than us having to hunt them. We can pay a fee and reserve the room for longer if we want to go again, or we can simply wait. The line wasn't so bad this time."

Luke laughed. "You mean not everyone wants to fight things on vacation, only us weirdos?"

Izzie cracked her knuckles. "It's exercise, not a fight."

A rumbling voice came from all around—one of the Kilomea staffers. "Attention, guests. The chosen scenario will begin in one minute. Please make any necessary preparations at this time."

Alison summoned a shield and shadow blade on instinct. The spells were already as automatic as breathing for her, but she smiled at the easier flow of magic. Being in a kemana still had a few advantages. Mason raised his wand and cast a few enhancement spells. Izzie cast her own defensive spell. Luke growled and shifted into a large wolf.

Huh. I'm more used to seeing a fox than a wolf, even though wolf shifters are way more common than nine-tailed foxes. It's funny how life works out.

"Ten, nine, eight, seven, six, five, four, three, two, one... scenario start."

A loud foghorn sounded. Bright flashes appeared in the sky, one after another in rapid succession. As the light subsided for each, it left a brown-winged, squat humanoid shape. Soon, dozens of the creatures hovered in the arena sky and their wings flapped gently. Alison narrowed her eyes. The bright sun shadowed her enemies, which made it hard to discern details. When she finally could, her brain refused to accept what she saw.

"Wait a second...are those..." She laughed. "It can't be. Mason, you're twisted."

He laughed. "I told you. The goal was silly, not realistic."

"But..." She gestured at the flock of creatures when words failed her.

Their opponents were fuzzy winged teddy bears with button eyes. They spread out in the sky and babbled in an unintelligible singsong manner.

Luke shook his muzzle and growled.

"Not exactly the stuff terror is made of," Izzie replied. She frowned and shook her head. "Or exactly the stuff terror is made of."

She was right. There was something almost more unsettling than if they had been surrounded by actual snarling monsters.

With my luck, in the future, I'll probably die after being eaten by a giant teddy bear.

Mason slid his wand into his holster and raised his fists. "Let me ask you something, A. Does this remind you of anything?"

"Not really." She barked out a laugh. "I've had a few weird jobs, but I have trouble remembering something similar to fighting winged singing teddy bears. This is like a weird kids' show written by someone who's high."

He bowed with a dramatic flourish. "Then I've done my job. I wanted you to cut loose, not remember recent jobs. It's easy. All we have to do is defeat all these teddy bears before the time limit is up. I wanted an easy scenario, but I did ask them to tweak a few parameters simply because it's us."

Alison raised her blade. "Giant bugs and teddy bears. It's been a crazy few weeks. I remember when the only thing I worried about was scaring away a few gang members from my neighborhood. When are they going to—"

The singsong babble continued while teddy bears on all sides dove toward the group, but the bulk of the adorable fuzzy army remained in the sky and simply maintained their current positions. She didn't bother with her wings and instead, planted her feet firmly to meet the enemy's swooped attack. The blade sliced easily through the first opponent and left two halves with white stuffing at her feet.

"They even have stuffing!" She laughed as she cut another enemy down. "Mason, you are so twisted."

Someday, I can see Thomas hating me for doing this.

His heavy palm strike careened a furry opponent away. "In my defense, they were already an option. I merely tweaked a few things. So, technically, the resort management are twisted."

Izzie blasted a target in the chest at point-blank range with a light bolt. The poor flying teddy spiraled before it thunked into a rusted car. Mason spun and kicked another that charged him. The blow hurled it back and it landed on the street. Luke bit into the throat of one and snarled when he received a mouthful of stuffing as a result. The defeated bears and their fluffy innards began to melt into a gray liquid that seeped into the ground. The first wave of enemies had been defeated.

This would have been weird even in a Louper match.

There was only a small window of respite before another group launched an assault on the friends. The tempo of their babbling had increased but not the intelligibility.

"Did they explain the magic they use for this place?" Alison asked as she decapitated one.

"Nope," Mason replied. He pounded his elbow into the neck of an enemy. "It said the spells used are proprietary. Are you thinking technomagic like the emitters in the tac room? That would make sense."

Luke leapt toward two bears. He bit into one and batted

the other while it was still airborne. When he landed, he ripped the second one open as it attempted to stand. Another barreled into him and managed to tackle him but the huge wolf removed its head as a reward for its bravery. He threw up his head and howled in victory.

Izzie snickered as she eliminated a few more of their opponents with quick blasts of light magic. "I feel like we're the bad guys in this scenario."

"Definitely." Alison skewered another plump furry body. "We're the villains from a kid's story. The Dark Princess and her Evil Guard—the Handsome but Nasty Wizard, the deadly Jasper Elf, and the Politician Werewolf."

Izzie and Mason both burst out laughing. The strangled growl that escaped Luke was the closest version he could manage in his current form.

The teddy bears ceased their assault. The survivors of their flock circled above, still communicated in their nonsensical and vaguely musical speech, and showed no hint of anger or concern other than the heightened speed.

"There's probably some teddy bear race on Oriceran that would be offended if they knew what we were doing." Alison grinned.

"Definitely." Izzie kept her arm raised and her palm up, ready to launch another attack.

The flying bears increased speed and now circled the group twice as fast as before. The entire flock plummeted and converged on them from every direction while their inane song increased in volume and tempo.

"Teddy bombing raid!" Alison shouted.

The elf flung explosive bolts in a wide arc and the sky filled with charred fabric while it snowed stuffing. Alison didn't release a spell but cleaved through several of the diving assailants with one swing. Other surviving bears pounded into her and actually strained her shield. A cloud of fuzzy paws and button eyes surrounded her.

They hit harder than I expected. No wonder those witches looked a little worse for wear, especially since it didn't sound like they were fighting winged teddy bears.

The attackers' numbers provided an advantage, but they presented little resistance to her shadow blade. Grunting, she swung and stabbed until she stood in a pile of stuffing and white wisps floated in the air around her and the toy carnage.

"Is everyone okay?" she asked.

"Fine. I think that's all of them." Izzie wiped the sweat off her brow. There was less stuffing around her but blackened teddy bears lay in piles nearby. They began to melt, along with the debris around Alison.

Mason punted a survivor away. "The scenario didn't call for additional waves. I should have made it more difficult but I didn't think we'd defeat them so quickly."

Alison frowned and pointed at the guys' melting piles. "Why did more come after us?"

"Dynamic difficulty adjustment," the life wizard explained with a grin. "I don't know how it works, but it seems like the arena considered you two a bigger threat."

Luke shifted into human form. He spat a few times and wiped his mouth. "Ack. That fuzz tastes awful. There is way too much stuffing still in my mouth."

The remains of the toys seeped slowly into the ground.

Alison laughed. "I never would have guessed that I'd start my vacation by massacring teddy bears."

CHAPTER TWELVE

In the aftermath of the War on Teddy Bears, the group returned to Alison's room to discuss their plans. Mason ducked into the bathroom for a quick shower, and Luke headed to his room to do the same, citing the particular need to wash his mouth out. Izzie told him she would follow soon to bathe, but she wanted to catch up with her friend for a few minutes.

Alison snickered from her perch on the bed, feeling genuinely relaxed for the first time since her arrival at the resort. "Every time we get together, something impressive and memorable happens. I don't know if what we did is impressive or merely strange, but at least it'll be memorable. It's like Mason said. I've fought many things but nothing like that."

"Definitely memorable. And it was fun." Her friend released a contented sigh from the couch. "This is what we both needed—to cut loose with nothing important on the line. No big enemy, no bounties, nothing. I feel so relaxed now, and if what Mason's saying is true, I want you to feel what I feel, Alison."

"I'm relaxed," she insisted. "And it's not like that anyway, Izzie. You're the last person who should feel sorry for me. I didn't have to hide for years like you did, and our situations aren't even remotely the same."

"Really?" Her expression hardened. "We went through so much together at the school, and the Seventh Order didn't exactly ignore you as an adult once you interfered with their plans. They attacked you, your city, and even your company. They could have killed most of your friends and employees. When I was on the run, I mostly only had to worry about myself, but you have all your people to worry about."

"I didn't say I had no trouble, only that our situations weren't the same, but that's the past. They're gone now." She forced a big smile on her face. "I have a fancy house and a business and a cute baby brother. You're still trying to claw back the life the Seventh Order stole from you."

"Spare me the relativism. Just because people's pain is different doesn't make it any less their pain." Izzie folded her arms. "If anything, I have it easier in some ways."

Alison's brow wrinkled and the confusion spread to the rest of her face. "Huh? That honestly doesn't make sense to me."

"I had one clear enemy to destroy," the other woman explained. "And now that I have, I have my life back. But you are always worried about the next big bad you have to confront, and you keep running into weird situations. It's not only that you have the entire company to fuel your Brownstone worries, but you end up in situations I would never end up in because of it. I still mess around with the occasional bounty, but it's rare that anything escalates."

"It's only Brownstone luck. We've been over this before. It's not a big deal." She chuckled. "Listen to us. Anyone else would think our lives are insane."

Izzie shrugged. "Aren't they? Just because we both adapted to our weird lifestyles doesn't mean they aren't any less bizarre. We both could use a little normalcy."

"Like what?" she asked.

"Maybe when you get married, you'll calm down," her friend suggested. "Let's stop the comparisons and focus on the good things coming up. Is there any progress on the wedding planning?"

Alison groaned. "No. Some good things are coming up later rather than sooner, I guess."

"Is Mason being difficult?"

"No, not at all." She shook her head. "It's not his fault. It's mine. I honestly don't know what I want. Big wedding. Small wedding. Earth wedding. Oriceran wedding. There are so many possibilities. Every time I think I have something pinned down, I question it or change my mind. I'm not one of these girls who spent her entire life planning the perfect wedding. I didn't even plan to get married this soon."

"I think most people don't have a solid plan for this kind of situation." Izzie tapped her heart. "This is what decides, right?"

"I guess. It's still annoying."

She smiled. "I'm not doubting that, but you're making it too hard."

"I'm honestly not trying to," Alison complained. "If I

knew how to simplify this whole process, I would. Do you have any suggestions?"

"A few, actually. Think about what would make you happy. A wedding's supposed to be a joyous occasion. I won't lie and say it'll be stress-free, but Mason obviously loves you and you love him, and that's the important part. It's not like Shay will disown you if you choose the wrong flower arrangement. I think she had an elaborate wedding as much to screw with your dad as anything."

"Basically, yeah. Mom does like to mess with Dad." Alison glanced at the bathroom door. For all the advanced magic of the resort, judging by the sound, water was piped in the old-fashioned way. "What about you and Luke? You've gone from claiming you weren't the same woman he once loved to exploratory dating and now going to expensive resorts with him. To be clear, I think that's a good thing. Ever since I saw the picture of you in his office, I knew he still loved you."

Izzie shrugged. "You got me. I tried to convince myself we couldn't pick up where we left off, but that's obviously not true. Even when I started going out with him again, I thought it wouldn't amount to anything but the feeling's still there, and this time, we aren't stupid kids. We're adults who have both been through a lot. We both know what we want from life and we both know all too well the dangers of who and what we are."

"You were kids who had been through so much before," Alison pointed out quietly. "Whatever we were toward the end of school, I don't think you could call us naïve."

"I don't know. Merely being around death and suffering isn't the same as understanding it. The Seventh Order helped me understand it in their own twisted way. But it does feel like..."

"Feel like what?" she asked.

The elf stared at her hands. "It feels like this might actually work. That it's not some ridiculous dream."

"That's because it isn't. You deserve to be happy, especially after everything you went through since the School of Necessary Magic." She scoffed. "Shit. You deserve to be happy because of everything you went through before going to the school."

"I know," Izzie whispered. She looked down and rubbed her hands together. "It's hard for me, Alison. It really is. The truth is, I forgot how to be happy when I was on the run. No. It's worse than that."

She frowned. "How?"

"It's not that I forgot how to happy. It's that I wouldn't allow myself to feel it, not really. I knew that if I let myself be satisfied and care about something other than survival for more than a moment, the people pursuing me would come and snatch it away. I was afraid for a while, even after they were destroyed, that I wouldn't be able to feel happiness again—that the Seventh Order's hunt had left me a twisted shell of a woman who didn't know how to do anything but survive day-to-day and hunt enemies."

"But that's not true. You know that, right? If you don't believe me, ask Luke. It doesn't matter that we care about you. We won't lie to you."

The elf's smile brightened her face. "Yes, I know it's not true. And you're right. I have so many things to live for now—things I couldn't dare risk before. I have friends and family I can freely see without worrying about dark wizards attacking them. I have Luke. I don't know what my future will bring but now, I see possibilities rather than endless darkness and hunts. I have a life again, thanks to your help."

"And does that future include a wedding?" Alison asked and her smile mirrored her friend's. "I'm not trying to push one way or another. I understand that you might need a long time to work everything out, but I can't help but be curious."

"Maybe. If he asks me, I think I'd say yes." Izzie nibbled on her lip. "Maybe that's stupid or ridiculous, but that's where I'm at. I don't want to pressure him either, so I'm willing to wait until he's comfortable. The love is there. I know that for certain, but we are still reacquainting ourselves with one another in so many ways."

"He'll ask you," she murmured. "He never stopped hoping you would come back to him, and he never stopped loving you. I bet he simply wants to give you space and make sure you're ready for it."

"We have time. That's the great thing about having a future and no major alliance of evil wizards targeting you. I don't feel so much pressure. It's wide-open now. So you go ahead and have your wedding first. That way, I can study all the failures and do the opposite."

"Very funny." She rolled her eyes. "For that, I should put you in charge of something annoying at my wedding."

The water stopped.

Izzie stood. "If Mason's done, Luke's probably close. We'll catch you later for dinner, okay?"

"Sounds good. We should be back in our room by 4:30."

She waved, headed out of the room, and closed the door quietly behind her.

Alison stared at the door, a soft smile on her lips.

Good friends, my fiancé, and teddy bear murder. What's not to like?

CHAPTER THIRTEEN

The two couples were close to the lobby and on their way back to their rooms after a pleasant dinner. Alison laughed, her face a little heated and her head faintly fuzzy from the wine she'd drunk.

It'd been a few days since her arrival at the resort, and she'd spent most of her time in the main resort area enjoying the amenities, including the arena, restaurants, pool, and even a small concert theater with an eclectic but talented small orchestra. She'd visited a few shops in the kemana nearby but mostly, she did what Mason wanted and didn't worry about doing anything except relaxing.

They had shared stories at dinner and finished with Alison detailing her last bounty trip with her father.

"It was gross," she exclaimed. "At the time, it didn't register as much, but when I thought about it later, I kept thinking about how messed up it was. It made me appreciate a straightforward humanoid enemy."

"Acid-blood giant bugs." Luke looked disgusted. "I don't

even know how I would handle that. It's not like I could bite them without hurting myself."

"Stay out of the bounty-hunting business and you'll be fine," she suggested.

Izzie grinned. "You're both missing the really twisted part of this."

"What?" she asked.

"The real craziness of this isn't that you had to fight a guy who summoned his giant bug swarm. It's that you thought it would be a good father-daughter bonding activity."

She snorted. "We've always liked doing bounties together since I was a teenager."

The response summoned an even bigger grin from her friend. "Think about what you said. I wasn't hunting bounties with my mother when I was a teenager."

Mason chuckled. "She is a Brownstone. I think they kick her out of the family if she doesn't meet her beatdown quota."

Luke chuckled. "You say that but her mother's now a professor and her father runs a restaurant."

"Exactly!" Izzie exclaimed.

"Oh, like you wouldn't go kick ass with your mom if she asked?" Alison challenged. "She basically invented modern magical bounty hunting. I know your dad's a strange case with the multiple-generation gap and everything."

The elf shrugged. "My mother and father can definitely take care of themselves, but they're a little less…whatever it is you want to call you Brownstones. Bloodthirsty?"

She laughed. "We're not bloodthirsty."

They all laughed together as they entered the lobby. It was fuller than usual and several groups of people huddled together and spoke in furtive tones. A wave of silence swept the room with the arrival of their group.

"We weren't that loud," Alison murmured. "They don't all have to look so offended."

Everyone turned to stare, including the employees at the check-in counter. She looked around the room. It was obvious they weren't staring at the group but specifically at her.

Okay, this isn't weird at all. What? Have you never seen a laughing Drow princess before?

She marched up to a haughty-looking Light Elf woman in an evening gown. Her disdain was so thick, she could almost taste it in the air.

"What?" Alison demanded. Maybe it was the alcohol, but she wasn't in the mood for crap. She'd come to the resort to relax, not have people get pissy because she laughed a little loudly.

The woman wrinkled her nose. "I owe you nothing, Drow." She turned and stormed off. "Shameful. Simply shameful."

What the hell is going on? Did something else happen? This can't be about us laughing.

She turned toward another person staring at her—one of the witches she had seen outside the arena a few days prior.

"Hey," she began, this time in a calmer tone.

"I'm sorry. I can't." The witch burst out laughing and ran off, her hand over her face.

Startled, she turned to her friends. They all shrugged and looked even more confused than she was.

Did some news site do a hatchet job article on me? Even if they did, no one here would likely have read it.

The Nicht bellhop emerged from the crowd and nodded toward an unoccupied space near the wall. She smiled but it didn't reach her eyes. "Can I speak to you, Miss Brownstone?"

She nodded and followed the woman. "Two hours ago, I went to have dinner and no one paid me any attention but now, everyone's looking at me like I threatened their mothers. I know I'm Alison Brownstone the Dark Princess and all that crap, but no one has cared until now. What gives?"

The woman cleared her throat and heaved a sigh. "I volunteered to talk to you about this and I do have to say that management does understand that when someone's under the influence, they can do unusual things. It's not like anyone was hurt in the incident, but still." She uttered a nervous chuckle. "But please, don't do it again. It'll make things complicated. We want you to have a pleasant time at the resort but we also have to think of the experience of other guests."

"What in the hell are you talking about?" Alison stared at the woman, her mouth a tight line. "I don't understand. What have I done that would have upset the other guests? Other than me yelling at the woman a few minutes ago, I've barely even looked at anyone, let alone scowled at them. And you have to understand, I scowl a fair amount normally."

"You've obviously been drinking. I can smell it on your

breath. That's fine, and you said you were having dinner two hours ago?"

"Yeah. What about it?"

The Nicht averted her eyes. "Did you have a few drinks before dinner, Miss Brownstone? Be honest."

"Tell me what's going on," she muttered through gritted teeth. "Because right now, I have no damned clue what's going on."

The woman placed her palms together in a pleading motion. "Please, Miss Brownstone. Although not all our guests belong to species with nudity taboos, given our location and primary client base, we can't have people flying around naked. Please consider this your official warning." She spun on her heel and hurried away, her face scarlet and her wings twitching.

She stood there with her mouth open and her heart pounding. "What the hell? Did she actually say flying around naked?"

An hour later, the friends reconvened in Luke and Izzie's room after a few quick questions of the crowd by Luke and Izzie. Alison, at Mason's suggestion, left to reduce the strange combination of tense staring and embarrassed snickering.

She lay on the couch, her head lolled back. "It can't be. Please tell me you made that all up."

The shifter's mouth twitched and the corners threatened to curl into a smile. "No, we asked several people. They all said the same thing. Alison Brownstone was flying around the gardens naked, laughing and obviously drunk."

"And this occurred allegedly fifteen minutes before we went to dinner?" she asked.

Izzie nodded. "Several people claimed to have seen the incident but not everyone paid attention to the time. We did find different people who did know the time, and they all seemed to agree about when it happened."

Mason sat in a chair, irritation etched on his face. "She was with me. I think I would have noticed if she stepped out for a little naked sky jaunt."

The elf held a hand up. "I know. I'm not saying Alison was drunk and flying around the gardens naked. To be honest, I don't think she's even capable of that. It'd require her to loosen up for far too long."

Luke snickered but had the decency to look abashed when Alison shot him a glare.

She took a deep breath and rubbed her temples. "As Mason pointed out to me earlier, I'm not the only woman on the planet with white hair. This place is crammed full of magicals, so why are they so sure it's me? One of the bell-hops is a Nicht. I've seen several Arpaks around and a few other winged species. That doesn't even take into account people flying with spells or illusions."

"Shadow wings," Izzie explained. "Several people had a good, direct look at you and normally, I'd say, 'So what?' But you're not me. You're someone who is in the news often and Drow are one of the few races that fly with those kinds of magic shadow wings. For that matter, elite Drow are one of the few that do. I double-checked, and there were a few people who probed during the incident and determined it wasn't an illusion."

Alison sat up. "I wasn't there. Someone obviously impersonated me."

"I know, Alison. I'm not saying magic wasn't involved, only that someone was actually up there, flying. It wasn't a projection or an illusion or an implanted memory." She shrugged. "I don't know anything more than that. If it helps any, people are mostly amused rather than angry, despite that one woman's attitude. Several people even said it changed their opinion of you."

She scrubbed a hand down her face. "I bet it did."

"They say you're more 'fun' than they realized."

"Just kill me now." She slumped in her chair.

Mason leaned forward and cupped her chin with his hand. "Impersonating a Brownstone is very dangerous, but all they did was embarrass you with a stunt. That means this might have simply been a joke—a stupid joke, but nothing more serious."

"It's not a joke," she insisted. "Put the pieces together. I saw *myself* the first day we were here—that woman who stepped into the elevator. I should have investigated instead of assuming I was wrong. Now, I'm apparently flying around naked where everyone can see me using magic associated with elite Drow. The conclusion is obvious."

"Is it?" Luke asked. "Because I'm not so sure."

She pounded her palm with her fist. "It's Drae, the Princess of the Deepest Night. She's come here to screw with me. I thought I was being watched earlier and now, it all makes sense. I was. She's probably keeping on an eye on me—or has people who are—so she can coordinate crap like that stunt." She scoffed. "I'll admit I didn't think this was how she'd operate, but at least she's not trying to hurt anyone yet. It doesn't mean I forgive her, though."

The other three all exchanged skeptical looks.

"Come on," Alison insisted. "It fits the available evidence. Do you have a better theory?"

"Maybe it does," Mason replied. "But we still don't know much. We know someone flew naked the other day above the garden, but did any of the witnesses verify it was actually shadow magic used to fly?"

Izzie furrowed her brow in concentration before she shook her head. "They confirmed it wasn't a pure illusion, but not much more. With all the background magic around the resort, it can be hard to confirm something like that without far more effort than they spent during a naked flying incident."

"If it is this other Drow princess, what does she hope to gain?" Luke asked. "Shouldn't that be the first question we ask? Do the Drow have strict rules about drunken nude flying? If that's all it took to win the throne, I doubt they would waste time with things like setting up fake jobs and attacking you. Everything you've told us about the struggle for the throne makes it seem that pure dignity isn't a major consideration with all the betrayals and lies."

"I hear what you're saying, but she's the main one who makes sense," Alison responded. "It might be that Drae thinks this will weaken me on Earth. It could be a prelude to something more."

"Or it's not Drae at all," Mason suggested. "It might be nothing more than a stupid prank by any guest here—a fun story to tell people when they go home. 'I saw drunken Alison Brownstone flying around naked. Isn't that crazy?'"

"We need to get to the bottom of this," she insisted. "If it's not merely some stupid prank and it is Drae, she might escalate to something more serious and she knows I won't be here for long. We need to probe deeper and ask around. Did you guys check with hotel security at all? The bellhop made it obvious the hotel staff believes I did it, but she didn't explain what evidence they have, if any."

"No. We didn't talk to them. Only people in the lobby." Izzie stood and rubbed her hands together. "You should talk to hotel security. The rest of us should spend more time asking around."

Mason nodded. "It sounds like a good plan, but A, if this turns out to be a stupid prank, we can handle this in a calm manner."

"I won't pull a Dad on them," she assured him. "I'll simply make them loudly explain how they're lying scumbags in the lobby. Clothing optional."

Luke's expression turned grave. "And if it is Drae? You can't fight a Drow princess here. I don't care if it's a resort full of magicals, most of these people haven't been within five miles of a real fight. People will get hurt, and if it's her, she might have brought help."

Alison sighed. "She's still a Drow princess in the end. If I challenge her directly, I doubt she'll say no, even if I put a few conditions on the battle. I merely need to corner her first. I can then take her to some far end of the kemana and finish this crap. But first, we need to find out what's actually going on. My money's still on her, but for all I know, maybe a Light Elf simply wants to embarrass a Drow."

Luke stood and moved beside Izzie. "We'll get to the bottom of this, Alison. Don't worry about it. I'm sure it'll be nothing important in the end."

The couple stepped out of the room and closed the door behind him.

"Damn it," Alison muttered.

Mason began to pace and a scowl marred his natural good looks. "I've warned you about not overreacting, but maybe I should warn myself."

"What?"

"I wanted you to have a relaxing couple of weeks and now, some idiot is ruining it. I don't think it's Drae, but it doesn't matter. Now we have to waste time with an investigation." He raised a fist. "We'll going to find this son of a bitch as soon as possible and we'll enjoy the rest of our damned vacation. Alison Brownstone, you will relax even if I have to pound a confession out of someone."

She scoffed. "One can dream, but before that, I need to have a little chat with security. This isn't only bad for my reputation. It's bad for their hotel if they allow people to impersonate other guests."

CHAPTER FOURTEEN

With a carefully pleasant expression on her face, Alison settled into a comfortable leather chair across from the frowning wizard in a suit. The man's beard and weathered face reminded her vaguely of her dark magic defense professor from the School of Necessary Magic, Xander Powell, but his desk nameplate confirmed a far different identity—Sebastian Colton, Head of Resort Security.

Okay, I can do this. I merely need to be smart about it.

"Good evening, Miss Brownstone," Sebastian drawled, a hint of the Deep South in his voice. "The on-duty clerk said you were rather insistent on speaking to security. If this is about the earlier incident, I thought it was made clear to you that we will not follow up, provided you don't create an additional ruckus. We understand these things can happen, but we still have standards here that we need to maintain, even for people of your wealth, fame, and background."

She took a deep breath and reminded herself what the

situation must look like from his position. A famous, rich, celebrity bounty hunter and security consultant came to his resort and decided she could do whatever she wanted. Her normal instincts wouldn't help. This wasn't her confronting a bounty or defending a client. Threats or arrogance would only feed into the misunderstanding.

I have all this magic but sometimes, the most direct ways of tricking people are still the most effective.

"Okay, here's the thing," she began. "I have a few questions because I can guarantee you that I definitely did not fly around drunk and naked earlier, and I have every reason to believe that someone used magic to frame me for that little incident."

He leaned back in his chair and folded his hands together. "I see. I won't claim that's impossible, but it also seems very elaborate and ill-considered, given your reputation. Do you have any proof that you've been framed? Because many people do things they later regret and then disavow them. I'm sure you've heard that a few times in your own career."

"That's why I'm here. I need to better understand the evidence. There has to be some kind of surveillance in the public areas, either magical or technological—or both— right? There's no way a place this high-end will simply rely on people behaving themselves."

"True enough." The wizard nodded, pity in his eyes.

He doesn't believe me at all. Damn it.

Alison took a deep breath. "About the security?"

"We actually use cameras for the public areas," Sebastian explained. "This includes the gardens, and yes, we do have footage of you from the incident if that what's you're asking. We have not relied solely on eyewitness testimony."

"Cameras? Not spells? Really? Huh. I didn't expect that."

He shrugged. "We found through experimentation when we first opened that it ends up easier to use cameras and in some ways, using out-of-sight cameras works better. You'd be surprised how often someone thinks to ward themselves but they forget about simple straightforward recording, especially when they can't see a camera. People assume too much, especially Oricerans who haven't been to Earth much." He chuckled. "Or maybe you wouldn't be surprised. I know you insist that you didn't do this, Miss Brownstone, but we do have considerable witnesses and footage. That's sufficient evidence to suggest you did have a little fun."

"But at the time I was allegedly flying around naked, I was in my room," she insisted. "And I went to dinner afterward."

"That's convenient to claim, but we don't record footage from inside rooms for obvious privacy reasons."

"But you record the hallways, right?" she asked. "You would have seen me coming and going. You must have footage of me leaving for dinner."

"But all of that assumes you didn't portal," Sebastian countered. "The rooms are warded well against most spying magic but not all types of magic. This is a resort, not a prison."

She sighed. Insisting she couldn't portal wasn't likely to sound convincing. How did one prove something to someone already inclined to not believe them?

"Do you think I could be so drunk that I would fly

around naked but somehow still manage portal spells?" she asked. "Doesn't that seem unlikely?"

"For most people, maybe, but most people aren't a half-Drow princess who can call on so much raw power. I wouldn't have been able to seal the Mountain Strider in Seattle, and I happen to consider myself a strong wizard, Miss Brownstone. You have accomplished much in these last few years that most magicals wouldn't be able to."

Alison groaned and face-palmed. "This is ridiculous. What about people who saw me in the restaurant later? If I was so blitzed, how could I have a relaxed time there?"

He uttered a hearty laugh. "Come now. Are you telling me you didn't use a little magic to sober up? I used to know a fellow who carried a potion specifically for that. He'd go out and drink himself half to death and use the potion. I'm sure it was still terrible for his liver."

She was running out of options. If the hotel staff were against her, it would limit her ability to follow-up on whatever was going on. A push too hard, and she'd end up ejected from the resort and would never find out who had impersonated her.

"Truth spell," Alison declared.

"Excuse me?" Sebastian leaned forward and a frown crept onto his face.

"I'm willing to submit to a truth spell," she elaborated. "I'll let you search me for artifacts, too. I didn't do it, and I'll do whatever it takes to prove it to you."

His careful gaze focused on her for an uncomfortably long time before he spoke. "I appreciate your willingness to go that far, but I don't know if it would prove anything."

"You'd know if I had any spells or magic on me before you did the truth spell. Why wouldn't it help?"

"Do you use truth spells a lot in your line of work?" he asked.

She shook her head. "I've used them before but they're not something I use often. Why?"

He gestured to a photo hanging on the wall. In it, he, along with several dark-suited men and women, stood with their wands out in front of a massive American flag hanging on the wall.

"Do you know what I did before I took the job here?" he asked.

"I didn't look into the security of the place that much to be honest," she admitted.

"I spent twenty years with the PDA." A wistful smile crept onto his face. "I've seen some of the worst magic has to offer. In that sense, I understand you and many of the things you've accomplished already. I still keep enough of an ear on the agency to know you've been helpful to them to Seattle." He shook his head lightly. "I'm not saying this to tell you I'm about to look the other way or any of that nonsense, but only to explain that I spent a long time dealing with things like truth spells and I quickly realized the best way for someone to beat one."

"A truth-bender?" she asked.

Sebastian chuckled. "Artifacts are the sloppiest way to beat something. Anything you can take away from someone isn't a good thing to rely on." He tugged on a lapel to reveal his wand holster. "This is why, in the end, people like you who don't need wands always have an advantage over people like me. No, Miss Brownstone, the best way to beat a truth spell is the most obvious. You beat it by not lying."

"Okay. I understand that, but I'm a little lost here. The whole point of the spell is to identify the truth, and I want to prove to you that I'm telling you the truth."

"The real question is what is a lie?" His eyebrows raised. "Have you ever run into that? The truth spell doesn't work if the person doesn't believe they're telling a lie. Maybe you don't remember flying around the gardens and so you wouldn't honestly be lying."

Alison folded her arms with a defiant frown. "Since you spent twenty years in the PDA, let me ask you my own question. Given everything I've said, what I'm willing to do, and the nature of the incident, does it make sense that I somehow wouldn't know that I did what I'm accused of? It doesn't only require me to be drunk and stupid but now, it requires me to be drunk, stupid, and do complex magic at the same time."

Sebastian's forehead wrinkled, and he sighed. "My instincts tell me to trust you and sometimes, those instincts are the real magic. I'll keep what we've discussed in mind if there's a future incident, but the hotel won't declare you weren't responsible without clear proof of someone else."

"Fine. At least we're making progress. May I watch the footage?"

He shook his head. "We give that to law enforcement only, but if you're willing to take the word of a former PDA agent and gentleman, I can tell you that whoever is on that video looks like you and uses magic that looks like yours. It's not crazy for us to have believed it was you."

She took a deep breath and stood. "Looking like my magic and being my magic are two separate things. But thanks, I'll get out of your hair now."

Fifteen minutes later, she walked along a narrow path between high rows of sunflowers of different colors. There might be some small clue in the garden that had been missed, especially since security obviously didn't want to perform a detailed follow-up investigation.

I guess I can't blame them. They aren't cops, only hotel security. This guy should know better given his history, but maybe he simply wants to do his job here and nothing more. And it wasn't like anyone was hurt.

Alison turned a corner and almost smacked into a woman in a white dress. It took a moment for her to recognize Jade, who yelped and leapt back.

"Oh, it's you," the woman declared, her hand over her chest and her cheeks flushed. "And you're here of all places. Interesting." She bit her lip and her gaze lowered. Her bottom lip quivered as if she tried to avoid smiling.

She groaned. "I didn't fly around here drunk and naked. Let me make that clear. There are all kinds of ways to use magic to look like someone else. Someone impersonated me, and I don't know why."

Jade's eyes widened and she threw a hand over her mouth. "Of course. It all makes sense. It didn't seem like something you would do. Everything I've read in the news makes you seem... How to put it this? Overly serious? No offense."

"That's better than being a weirdo who flies out drunk and naked." She shook her head. "I'm hoping it's merely someone having a little fun, but I don't like the idea of someone impersonating me."

"Isn't that against the law?"

"Yeah." She looked up as if she might spot her naked doppelganger. "But this is a good place to try that kind of thing."

"A resort? Why? Wouldn't they care more about people breaking the law?"

Alison shook her head. "This is a resort but it's sitting in a kemana. Things are still rather different in kemanas. Non-federal law enforcement has no real jurisdiction here, and the local cops tend to be far more hands-off non-serious crimes than most modern people are used to."

"That's kind of cool and scary at the same time," Jade declared. "But I hope you find whoever is doing this, Alison. I remember in high school someone went streaking and blamed it on me. It took forever to convince people."

"Thanks. I only hope I can find them before they do something even more embarrassing."

CHAPTER FIFTEEN

The next afternoon, Alison shoved her wooden fork into her takeout container and twirled up the light-colored noodles. Brown paper bags littered the coffee table, all from a café called Happy Grains not that far from the resort. She didn't dare visit a resort restaurant or risk leaving the establishment until she had better clarity on the situation. Even room service was questionable. Someone might interfere with the employee on the way to her room. Instead, she'd taken advantage of a nearby café run by a chipper Wood Elf recommended by the front desk. Izzie and Luke had run out to grab the food and now, everyone had reconvened in her room to discuss the situation after an evening and morning of investigation.

Izzie grinned as she took a bite of a thick slice of dark bread. She swallowed. "Alison, you and me trying to solve problems. I'm having flashbacks to school, good and bad."

Mason eyed Alison with a smile. "It would have been interesting to know her then."

The elf shook her head. "There's no big mystery. She's the same other than being a little crankier."

Her friend frowned. "Crankier?"

"Sure." She grinned. "But the important stuff isn't any different. You care about others. Maybe too much, but let's talk about that later. We're here to go over the evidence."

"Sightings," Alison declared. "That's what you mentioned before, and that's what Mason told me about."

Luke frowned. "Yes. Everyone's been jabbering about the garden thing, but that's not the only weird thing you allegedly did since arriving. What I've heard from most people is that they simply assumed you were drunk."

Izzie finished swallowing another bite of her bread. "One guy said you offered him money to streak. He was too embarrassed to mention it until the garden incident. Another person said you made rude comments about non-magicals."

"What the hell?" She set her takeout container on the coffee table. "I'm not a magical supremacist. I've fought tons of people who are!"

"I know, Alison. I know. And it's not even like they claim you said something over-the-top hateful, only stupid jokes."

She sighed. "Do I even want to know?"

"For example, how many humans does it take to change a light bulb?"

"How many?"

"One, but they're lame because they have to use light bulbs instead of a spell." Izzie shrugged. "Like I said, stupid jokes. They make you sound like an idiot more than anything."

"Gee, I'm so glad to hear that. I feel so much better now."

Mason glanced toward the closed curtains that blocked their view of the garden. "I've talked to a few different staff who say Alison offered them autographs if they did stupid stunts. One maid said she offered her an autograph and money to throw herself in the fountain and declare herself 'The Last Disciple of The True Rhazdon.' One of the Kilomea at the arena claimed she stumbled past and asked if there were special adult settings on the arena simulator." He made air quotes around the world adult.

"I found a few people who merely described you saying weird, random stuff," Izzie reported. "Like one gnome who said you demanded he help you compose a new jingle for the company. Another woman said you were asking where your pet octopus was and crying about missing him."

Alison scrubbed a hand over her face. "I will kill whoever did this. I will fly over the garden with my clothes on, holding the imposter, and when everyone has had a good look at them, I'll fly a little higher and drop them."

"The big problem I see," Mason interjected, "is that the incidents have happened more often from what I can tell, including at least one after the garden incident last night."

"Why didn't anyone say anything before?" she asked. "Why didn't they care before the garden episode? We finally have the explanation for why I've felt I was being watched sometimes. It's probably all the people pointing and laughing about crazy, drunk Alison Brownstone, the Dark Princess crying for her pet octopus."

Omni can't turn into an octopus, can he? I'll have to remember to ask Hana.

"I think they didn't say anything for the same reason they wouldn't if someone impersonated me," Luke suggested. "You're a famous person with power and money and many people admire you, but they're also a little scared of you. If you thought one of the most powerful magicals in the country wandered around drunk and being stupid, would you want to piss her off by embarrassing her? And if they're not afraid of you, they're afraid of your father."

She stood and paced in front of the coffee table. "Do we know exactly when any of these happened? Mason mentioned one after the garden fiasco, and for that, at least, I know where I was." She pointed to the floor. "Here."

"It's not like everyone knew an exact time," the shifter responded, "at least for the people I talked to. But for one of the incidents described to me, you were having lunch with us at the time."

Mason nodded. "There were a couple that occurred when you were in the room with me."

"So the imposter isn't always that careful," she mused.

Luke took a deep breath and stared at her. "There's no such thing as a Drow shadow soul, right?"

Alison stopped and turned toward him, her head tilted in confusion. "Shadow soul?"

"It's not like some dark, kooky side of you spontaneously came into being because you're in the kemana? Anything like that?"

"I've never even heard of anything like that," she replied. "And come on. You of all people know this isn't my first time in a kemana, and I've been to Oriceran. If there was some weird side-effect of my mixed heritage that came with being in a higher-magic environment, you would have thought it would have appeared there. If that was remotely a danger, Myna, Rasila, or Miar would have mentioned it—or any of the Drow I trained with on Oriceran."

"I've read about a concept like that in Japan," Izzie explained, "but I'm not sure if it actually happens or if it's only a myth. It's hard to know these days."

Mason marched over to the curtains and pulled them open. He surveyed the garden, his face pensive. "Given the public reputation of the Brownstones, people wouldn't be shocked if Alison went to someone and threatened to kill them."

"Hey!" she yelled.

"It's not what I think, A." He shrugged. "I'm only saying that between you and your dad, people think you're more ruthless than you are."

"I get it," Izzie said suddenly. "You're wondering why everything we've found is so low-key and stupid. Someone could have walked around as Alison and threatened to kill people. Instead, they act like an idiot drunk. It's more like they're trying to embarrass her than destroy her."

"If they push too hard, the staff would have to eject me," Alison pointed out. "The security chief only mentioned the garden incident, so that suggests people haven't reported the other incidents to security, not even the staff members."

"You don't stay at many fancy places, do you, Alison?" Luke asked.

"After this, I'm not convinced I'll stay in any," she grumbled.

"The thing is, we're asking around about you, but I

guarantee there are many people who do stupid things. If staff had security threaten every drunken guest, this place would be empty in a few weeks." He shrugged. "Money and power talks. It's terrible, but low-level staff are expected to put up with rich people's bullshit."

"What about other rich people, though?" she countered.

He shook his head. "It's not worth starting a big scene over minor crap. They might even think it's leverage for the future."

Mason closed the curtains. "Should we take all this evidence to security?"

"I doubt it'll help," Alison replied. "I have the feeling the head of security believes me but that he also doesn't want a big investigation."

"That makes sense," Luke agreed. "A few of us asking questions because we're curious guests is one thing, but a formal security investigation—let alone getting the police involved—will harm this place's reputation. He might even ask you to leave if you push too hard on the investigation. The last thing they want is negative attention."

Izzie fished around in one of the paper bags for bread but found none. "We know someone's messing with Alison, but we still don't know who."

"Drae," Alison declared without hesitation. "It has to be her. She's the only one who makes any sense. It's not like I don't have other enemies, but most of them wouldn't waste time with this crap or they'd take advantage of my absence to attack Brownstone security. She's probing me, testing me, and maybe even testing Earth. A resort in a kemana is a good place to do it because it's closer to Oriceran culturally than a surface city."

Mason nodded, looking apologetic. "I thought you were being paranoid before, but I was wrong. I should have trusted your instincts. If you say it's Drae, I believe you, but I don't know what good that does us."

"We proceed with that assumption as we investigate." She frowned. "If it is her, it's unlikely she'll try to assassinate me directly, but she might try to target one of you."

Izzie snorted. "Then I'll show her that you don't mess with a Berens."

Luke's eyes flashed yellow for a moment. He uttered a quiet growl. "She might try Izzie, but I doubt she'll risk me."

"Why do you say that?" Alison asked.

"A Drow assassinating a US congressman is basically asking for war," he explained. "And she's taking advantage of the fact that the security here doesn't want to investigate too closely. If I die, the FBI, PDA, and innumerable other people might get involved. If there's a risk of interplanetary war, the Fixer or King Oriceran might even get involved."

"My father has access to enough spells to identify a true culprit easily," Izzie explained.

Mason nodded. "That all makes sense. If this was only about picking off people close to Alison, she would have already done it. If anything, priming her by pulling all these stunts makes it less likely she could get away with assassinating someone in disguise, not more."

She scoffed. "So the bitch is simply screwing with me to piss me off?"

He shrugged. "It's not like the Drow princesses don't

have a history of that. Rasila lied to you and her people attacked us as a test."

"Ugh. We need more information." She rubbed her temples and closed her eyes. "I think as long as I'm here, all she'll do is pull stupid tricks, but we can't watch the entire resort. There will always be an opportunity to make a scene when I'm somewhere no one else can see me."

"What are you thinking, A?"

"It could be about trying to embarrass me away from the resort." She gestured toward the window. "This place isn't a fortress but it is locked down in many ways. There is a heavy concentration of influential magicals, and it has decent security. She might be worried about starting something here and having it blow up in her face."

Mason frowned. "Do you think she'll make a move if you leave?"

"Yeah. Exactly."

"That's it?" Izzie scowled. "You'll simply run because some Drow princess is messing with you? You should stay here and fight."

Alison shook her head. "Not run. I'll merely give her an opportunity to up her game. She's not all that subtle, so if I do something like that, she might expose herself directly and we can end this quicker."

"And how do you intend to do that?" Her friend's expression suggested she thought the plan was a terrible idea.

"Easy. It's the resort that's locked down, not most of the kemana. We can take a little trip into town and see if something happens. She must have spells or spies monitoring the main resort buildings to track my movements. Otherwise, she wouldn't have been able to time her crap so well." She stood and cracked her knuckles. "The worst thing that happens is more rumors of me being stupid and drunk."

CHAPTER SIXTEEN

The buildings of the resort towered above the shorter kemana buildings, even at a distance. Densely packed smaller wooden and stone buildings clustered around the central hotel like an unruly lawn. The dusty, narrow roads were all but empty now that Alison and her friends had cleared the lively zone of shops and restaurants around the resort.

Near the tourist center, one might believe the kemana was a thriving urban environment filled with commerce, joy, and the occasional interesting Willen puppeteer. The mask had fallen now.

A good number of the stores in this part of town stood empty. Unadorned windows exposed their empty interiors, the occasional cracked façade visible. Every once in a while, suspicious men or women watched the group from the shadows or a desperate-looking shopkeeper or restaurant owner stepped out from the front of their store to encourage patronage. A sign hung on the front door of a potions shop.

We're not listed on your resort guide because we refuse to pay them kickbacks.

"I've never been to a kemana like this before," Alison murmured. "It's not as bad as what happened in Seattle but it's almost sadder in a way. A few of the employees mentioned the resort helping keep this place alive, but it's surprising that only a few decades of open magic have wounded places like this so quickly."

"Magic doesn't mean anything if half your population has moved out." Mason walked beside her. "A little extra background magic isn't worth all the inconvenience of living in a place like this. It's not like all the kemanas will disappear, but these..." He sighed. "It's only a matter of time. At least a place like Ruby Falls has a major magical school to help keep it important. Why live in the equivalent of a small town underground when you don't have to?"

"It's not all that different than many non-magical small towns," Luke commented. "Post-industrialization forced a lot of changes. This is a similar situation."

Alison sighed. "All the more reason to take care of this problem without risking the resort. I don't want to add 'kemana killer' to my list of achievements."

They continued along the twisting, narrow roads of the kemana. There were fewer occupied buildings, and the suspicion in some people's eyes turned to sneering avarice.

Oh, come on. Please don't mess with us. You won't win and we have other things to take care of.

A man in a cloak stepped out of an alley and his hand moved to a wand at his belt. His eyes narrowed on Alison before he lowered his hand and retreated into the shadows.

"Good call," she shouted.

He grunted and fled deeper into the alley.

Izzie chuckled. "I'd say that's terrible, but there were many sketchy assholes in Ruby Falls and that place is still fairly healthy."

"I have no interest in a confrontation with a local thug," Alison explained. She stopped, turned, and looked in the direction of the resort. The main building was barely visible now. "But we've walked for a while. Drae's probably already made her move by now." Her breath caught as a pulse surged through the area. "Did you guys feel that?"

Izzie and Mason nodded.

Luke frowned. "Magic?"

"Yeah," she replied. "Everything's not drowning in enchantments out here like at the resort. It's a little easier to sense things, but that was still a big spell, whatever it was. I can't tell for certain, but it felt like it might have come from the general direction of the hotel."

No smoke poured from the location to billow out and fill the air near the massive cavernous roof of the kemana. There were no explosions or large portals feeding hordes of deadly monsters—or none they could see from so far away.

"Maybe we should head back," she suggested and now imagined a huge vengeful dragon laying waste to the kemana from the garden.

"I agree," Mason replied, his voice tight.

After nods from Luke and Izzie, the group turned to move up the street. Another two quick pulses of magic passed through the area.

Alison's heart rate kicked up. Bile rose in the back of her throat. She slowed and studied their surroundings for any sign of trouble. The empty street mocked her concern, but she layered a shield over herself anyway.

"I don't like this," she muttered.

"I think you have the right idea, A." Mason retrieved his wand for a few quick enhancement spells.

Izzie snickered. "We all came here for a vacation and now, we're getting ready for an ambush. I'll leave such a nasty review online."

Luke's eyes turned yellow. "If someone's planning an ambush, it's a big mistake." He shifted to wolf form and uttered a long, menacing growl before he sniffed the air.

The cobblestones of the road cracked and wood warped on surrounding buildings. Pieces spiraled away from the source to twist and warp until they formed headless men with sharped, pointed arms. An army now surrounded them.

"I could go for a few teddy bears about now," Alison commented. She flung her arm out and launched a sharp, thin shadow crescent. Her attack sliced through one of the wooden men, and the magical creation collapsed into nothing more than a lifeless heap of wood.

At least there's no one around to get hurt.

Izzie's light blast exploded against one of the cobble men and blasted chunks of rock away from its chest. A bright fireball streamed from Mason's wand and impacted with the same animation. The combined assault blew a smoking hole through the figure and crumbled into a pile of rocks. Luke pounced on one of the wooden men, biting and scratching. His opponent tried to slice his side but he'd ripped it in half before it had the chance to inflict any damage.

The life wizard pointed his wand toward Alison and shouted a spell. The road buckled and folded back on itself to form a natural barrier and slow the advance of more wood and cobble men. They clambered over the new barrier, nevertheless, and reached the top, where her deft attack decimated them.

Izzie grinned, swept her arm in an arc, and murmured a spell. A thin layer of ice formed across the street. Several of the enemies on her side slipped and fell. A small number of them were already close enough to escape the trap. Luke bounded into the nearest wood man for a little extensive carpentry while Izzie lobbed explosive orbs into their rocky cousins.

Two cobble men leapt from the top of the barrier toward Alison. She annihilated one with a double blast of light magic. The other pounded into her and fell but it generated only a slight sting and left her shield unchallenged.

She twisted toward her opponent and brought her free hand up to form a shadow blade. It sliced through the stone with ease and reduced it to rubble.

The enemy's superior numbers didn't make up for poor tactics and the strength of the team. The four fell quickly into a smooth, cohesive rhythm to make short work of the aggressors. The army soon succumbed and reverted to their source. Thick dust choked the air and piles of rock, along with bent and burned wood, lay scattered across the ground.

Izzie knelt beside Luke. Blood seeped from a jagged gash in the wolf's side. She placed her hand near the injury and a moment later, light suffused the wound and it sealed itself.

Alison released her blade and shield. After a quick spell to unfold the road, she shook her head. "I expected something to happen, but not that."

The shifter returned to human form and dusted wood chips off his shoulder. "You didn't expect to get attacked?"

"Not like that. Something feels off about it." She kicked a pile of stones that had once been a cobble man. "Or maybe that's part of her plan."

Mason turned slowly to survey the damage around them. They'd restored the main road but creating the army had left numerous potholes and gaping wounds in the nearby buildings.

"Should we wait for the kemana police?" he asked.

She shook her head. "I doubt they have more than a handful of cops in this place from what we've seen." She pointed to the resort in the distant. "Sometimes, attacks aren't always about killing people."

Izzie hissed. "Sometimes, they're about delaying people."

Alison snorted. "Exactly. Let's head back to the resort to find out what ridiculous thing I allegedly did now."

CHAPTER SEVENTEEN

By the time they returned, the front of the vast main central hotel of the resort was filled with chattering people. The huge crowd—both guests and kemana residents—lingering outside the front of the main resort building wasn't a good sign. Tension, concern, and fear etched the faces in the crowd.

"Damn it," Alison muttered. "What now? Mason and I did naked painting in the pool?"

The life wizard ground his teeth in frustration. "We'll find out what happened here and then we can go to the cops about the attack. Whatever the hell is going on, we're now far beyond pranks."

Alison pushed forward, her friends right behind her, and the crowd parted to let them through. A few people whispered and some gasped and turned away once they realized who it was. No one snickered, laughed, or pointed. Several witches and wizards lowered their hands toward their wands.

"I don't think it was a stupid prank this time," she murmured.

The Light Elf woman she'd questioned the day before tilted her chin, her eyes narrowed not in haughty disdain but pure disgust. Jade stood near the front of the crowd, her cheeks puffy and her eyes red.

"I can't believe it." The woman sniffled. "It wasn't supposed to be this kind of vacation."

Two hotel employees, a wizard, and a Kilomea stood on either side of the main doors. The frosted glass—along with a spell, Alison suspected—hid the lobby. They stared at Alison for a moment before they exchanged concerned glances.

"Go right in," the Kilomea rumbled. "They're expecting you. But maybe your friends should stay here."

"Why is that?" she asked.

His nostrils flared. "As if you don't know, Drow."

Mason squared his shoulders but that still left him dwarfed by the huge Oriceran. "We're not leaving her alone. We were attacked in town."

"Attacked?" The Kilomea looked dubious. "Whatever. You can work that out with everyone inside. But don't try anything."

Alison sighed. "I have the feeling this is way worse than naked flying." She stepped toward the doors and they slid open.

Two dark-uniformed wizards from the local police chatted to Sebastian and gestured toward a hallway. Several other members of the security team stood in the lobby but no guests were present.

One of the kemana police, a bearded man, turned

toward her and cleared his throat. "This simplifies matters. And here I thought she might have already fled to Seattle."

"Oh?" she asked and strode forward. "And why would I do that? I have a crime to report, but apparently, something important has happened here."

Sebastian looked at her and shook his head lightly as if to tell her not to resist what was coming next.

You should have stuck to pranks, Drae.

"We'd like to take you into town to question you, Miss Brownstone," the police officer explained.

He kept his wand pointed at her. His partner alternated between Mason, Izzie, and Luke. The hotel security didn't have their wands out. Sebastian maintained a blank expression, faint weariness in his eyes.

All that time I've put in with the Seattle PD doesn't mean shit here on the opposite side of the country in a kemana. Great. To them, I'm simply the Dark Princess, barely one step above a rogue Drow.

"Can you tell me what this is about?" she asked and managed to keep her tone polite and her hands hanging loosely at her sides. She couldn't attack cops, even if they were letting themselves blame the wrong Drow for whatever was going on.

"There was a murder about a half-hour ago," the bearded police officer explained, his voice quiet. "And you're the prime suspect, Miss Brownstone."

Alison hissed a sharp breath. "She's gone too far. If she wanted me to stay away from her, this was the stupidest way to do it."

"Who?" The cop narrowed his eyes. "Is there another victim?"

"I didn't kill anyone," she shouted.

The cop scoffed. "It's not like you've never killed anyone."

"I didn't kill anyone here."

"We have to ask you to come with us." The police officer slid his free hand into his pocket and produced a pair of handcuffs embedded with white crystal—anti-magic cuffs. "You're not under arrest yet. We merely need to ask you a few questions. These are as much for your protection as ours. Things are tense and a few precautions will make everyone feel more comfortable about this situation."

Mason stepped forward, his eyes narrowed and his teeth gritted. "She's not going anywhere with—"

She threw her arm up in front of him. "You only want me? And we'll start with questions, not arrests?"

"Yes," the police wizard replied but looked at Mason instead of her. "If you're innocent, coming with us to answer our questions will clear this up quicker. Unless you have something to hide, of course."

"Fine." She put her wrists together. "I surrender."

Izzie frowned. "Can't you do anything, Luke?"

"I don't have authority here," he answered. "And I assume they'll call the FBI and PDA. That would be my suggestion."

The cop looked at him with a faint smirk. "Oh, the big-shot shifter politician. Don't you worry. We may be a smaller kemana but that doesn't mean we're bumpkins here."

"It's okay, Izzie." Alison sighed. "Let me handle this."

"Are you sure?" The elf pointed toward the front door.

"The real killer could be in that crowd, watching and laughing under her breath."

"I'm sure she is, but the last thing we need to do is piss the local cops off."

The officer chuckled. "Good attitude, Brownstone." He glared at Izzie and Luke. "Listen to your friend unless you want to be taken in too."

The shifter's mouth twitched. "Don't threaten us."

"No threats, Congressman. I'm only doing my job." He holstered his wand and stepped toward Alison, the cuffs at the ready.

"You didn't do anything, A!" Mason shouted. "You've been framed."

She nodded. "The last thing we need to do is escalate things and distract the security and cops. If it is Drae who killed someone, she might kill more people. I need you all here to help protect the hotel. I'll work things out with the police. And under no circumstances do you contact my parents or Hana. I don't want anyone to get any stupid ideas."

Alison grimaced and imagined her dad on a rampage through the kemana, or Hana ripping through ten men with her claws while Angry Omni wreaked devastation behind her.

I can't even go on vacation without getting screwed over. I should have simply hung a hammock in my backyard.

Mason clenched his hands into fists. "And if you don't work it out?"

"Then it won't be the first time a Brownstone ends up in court." She sighed.

The police wizard muttered something under her

breath. "Put your arms behind your back," he ordered. When she complied, he snapped the cuffs on.

You've gone too far, Drae. Too damned far and I'll make you pay for it.

Thirty minutes later, Alison sat on a stone bench in a tiny barred cell. The police station itself was so unimpressive, her master bedroom was almost as big. The only halfway impressive feature was the complex glyphs that covered the bars and the floor in front of the cell. The air felt heavy and the magic radiating from the glyphs was oppressive. Even with her power, she'd have trouble drawing on her abilities.

The front door to the station opened and the bearded police wizard entered. He'd introduced himself as Constable Iritrin on the way to the station. As she suspected, the local kemana police force was tiny and only fielded a grand total of five constables.

"Did you have a chance to investigate it?" she asked and hiked one of her legs up on the bench. She rested her hands atop her knee. "We fixed the road before we returned to the resort, but there had to be other evidence there."

If Drae were killing someone at the resort, she couldn't have been waiting in the kemana to erase the signs of the fight.

"Yes, we found an area in the old shopping district that had been trashed," the constable replied. "But that doesn't prove that some mysterious army of puppets attacked you and your friends. Maybe you decided to destroy the town because you didn't care." He chuckled. "But let's go over your story. You claim some Drow assassin or a Drow princess is framing you for murder because of some politics over on Oriceran?"

"Yes. That's exactly what I claim."

"I can't say that's an excuse I've heard before." He stared at her for a moment while subtle emotion played across his face that she couldn't interpret.

"Even if you don't believe me and think I merely vandalized abandoned buildings, that damage proves we were there. You're cops. At a minimum, since it's so fresh, you can probably at least establish a time for the damage. How am I supposed to have murdered someone in the kemana and trashed the town at the same time?"

Constable Iritrin stroked his beard. "There are many ways, as I see it. You could have murdered the man and portaled away. Maybe this is your thing—you trash places after you kill someone. I know they let you get away with all kinds of things at home, but this isn't Seattle now, is it, Brownstone?"

"I can't portal." She shrugged. "Ask the Seattle PDA field office if you don't believe me. They can confirm it, and unless you think I have the federal government under my thumb, that should be proof enough."

"There are all kinds of spells and artifacts out there. Even if you can't portal, it doesn't prove anything. Besides, do you really expect me to believe a woman as powerful as you can't portal?"

Alison dropped both feet to the floor. "I'm working on it, but it's not a spell I can accomplish for idiosyncratic personal reasons." She took a deep breath and tried to calm her pounding heart. "Who did I allegedly murder?"

"We're still identifying the victim and trying to account for all the guests. Your attack incinerated him completely and we're working with the hotel staff to identify him." The constable whistled. "The way you charged up and blasted him, I'm surprised the crater's so small. The resort staff always brag about how reinforced that place is, but your little experiment proved it."

"I didn't kill anyone."

"So you say."

"And this was supposed to be only questions."

He shrugged. "We're talking. You're not under arrest. Yet. That's still as true as it was earlier."

She scoffed. "Isn't this all somewhat convenient? I've murdered someone and you don't even know who it is? For all I know, the whole thing was an illusion."

"We have multiple witnesses and footage that assure us it wasn't," he replied. "And that crater's not an illusion."

"I want a truth spell," she demanded. "You already searched me. You know I don't have any artifacts on me. You know I don't have any active enchantments. I didn't do it and this is a kemana. That should be enough to convince you."

"Fine." Constable Iritrin smiled. "You're right. That will simplify things. The hotel staff is reluctant to get involved, but we'll contact specialists from the PDA soon enough. They'll be able to better recover and determine exactly what kind of magic was used at the crime scene. And sure, if you pass the test, I can cut you loose but we'll have to take you out that cell to do it. So wait a minute. There's no way I'll do that without precautions."

She sneered at him. "If I wanted to escape, wouldn't I have done it at the resort?"

"Maybe, but that doesn't mean I have to be stupid about this." His expression darkened. "You'll have to wait until I get a few of my friends to help me."

I miss Agent Latherby.

A few minutes later, Alison stood outside the cell in cuffs while three shielded wizards pointed wands at her and Constable Iritrin chanted the truth spell. A large glowing white orb appeared in front of him with a pop.

"To be clear," he began, "my spell stays white if you tell the truth and it turns black if you lie. Do you understand?"

"I understand," Alison replied.

"Let's make sure it's working," he suggested. "State your name."

"Alison Brownstone."

The orb remained white.

"State your job," the constable ordered.

"I'm a security contractor." She rolled her shoulders. This would all be over soon, but she wasn't sure how to proceed after the police released her. She had mentioned Drae but using Earth authorities—even in the kemana—to help her locate a Drow princess seemed like a diplomatic nightmare waiting to happen. The best bet was for her to leave the resort, contact Rasila and Miar, and brainstorm a response.

I spent all that time trying to be neutral, but in the end, I couldn't get away from it. Damn it. Maybe Dad had the right idea. Go in, kick ass, and leave.

"I need you to tell me a lie," the constable stated. "Lie about your age."

"I'm twelve years old," she muttered.

The orb turned black. About five seconds later, it reverted to white.

"Good." Iritrin smiled. "Everything seems to be in working order. Let's get to the real question. Did you murder a man at the resort earlier today?"

"No." She punctuated her response with a furious shake of her head. "I need you to hurry up and cut me—" She gasped and her eyes widened. It couldn't be.

The orb turned solid black.

"Wait," Alison stammered. "What? That's impossible."

He sneered. "You thought that if you asked for a truth spell, we'd let you go, didn't you? We called your bluff, murderer. Don't worry. We'll let your friends know not to wait up for you."

CHAPTER EIGHTEEN

Mason slammed his fist onto the coffee table in his room. The hotel staff and police had allowed everyone to return to their room shortly after hauling Alison off. None of the guests appeared worried now that the police had made an arrest.

"We shouldn't have let her go with them," he complained. "Whoever set her up must have found a way to mess up a truth spell."

"We could easily break her out," Izzie suggested from beside Luke on the couch. "The police here are a joke."

Luke sat stiffly, his arms folded. "We can't attack police officers, Izzie."

"I'm not saying kill them, merely knock them out." She shrugged. "Alison's a sitting duck in that cell."

"If we break Alison out, she'll have to go on the run," he pointed out. "Do you really think that's for the best? You know what that's like."

She sighed and looked away. "I don't like the idea of doing nothing."

The life wizard growled. "I'm not crazy about it either. If this is Drae, maybe she'll try to eliminate Alison when she's at the station. A Drow princess will cut through those kemana cops like they're freshmen at a magic school."

Luke shook his head. "Everything Alison explained points away from an assassination, and I don't care if this is a Drow princess. Once the PDA starts seriously looking into things, they'll be able to establish that Alison didn't do it even if the local yokels can't. I'll check to make sure agents with good reputations are assigned to the case, but there's only so much I can push given my links to her. We don't want to give Drae more rope to hang her with. The more irregularities, the longer it'll take to clear this up."

Izzie stood and walked to the window. She threw the curtains open and glared out at the garden. "The naked flying prank happened out there, as did the murder. They've blocked off the area near the murder site, but not all of it. We should do a little investigation ourselves. If Luke is right, I don't think the murder was the final plan."

"You don't?" Mason asked.

She shook her head. "If the PDA can easily establish that Alison isn't guilty or if she simply passes their truth spells, this whole thing will fall apart. This makes me think that the murder is merely a fancier version of the ambush. A delaying tactic, but a delay for what? There's something else they want to accomplish. Something else they don't want her around to help with."

"But Alison's one woman—a powerful woman, but it's not like isolating her guarantees anything." Mason gritted his teeth. "What are they planning? More murders? That wouldn't make any sense. It'd prove she didn't do it, and this place would empty within hours."

Izzie turned and leaned against the wall, her arms folded. "They could set us up for murder next. We've been around Alison for days. Anyone watching her has to know we're important to her if they don't already."

"But they haven't faked us going around causing trouble," he observed. "They put far more effort into priming people to believe Alison might escalate her behavior."

Luke stared at the ground for a moment before he jerked his head up. "What if we're wrong?"

The other man glared at him. "You think Alison's a murderer?"

"No, no. Not that." He closed his eyes, took a deep breath in through his nose, and breathed out slowly before speaking again. "We've simply assumed that Alison's right. That this Drae is the one behind all of this."

"Alison might be paranoid, but she was right to be. She thought something smelled from the beginning. I'm inclined to trust her instincts on this."

Luke nodded. "Sure, but this Drow princess isn't the only person who might want to target her, and we don't even know if this plan is part of actually eliminating her. This doesn't smell like the kind of thing some manipulative Drow schemer would do. It's a little sloppy for that."

"How the hell is framing someone for murder not trying to take them down?" Mason's fingers twitched into fists.

"Because they have to know it won't stick," the shifter explained. "If they have the magic and patience to pull off everything that's happened, they aren't merely idiot street thugs or low-level punks with wands. Does a random Drow princess really believe she can defeat another Drow princess using local hick cops? Just because they can wave a wand around doesn't mean they can investigate a crime."

"It could be a test. Maybe Drae's trying to push Alison to see how much she'll take until she lashes out."

"No, it's a simple delay tactic, like Izzie said," he insisted. "But a sloppy one. I suspect this has nothing to do with the Drow. The magic we dealt with in town didn't seem very Drow-like either."

Izzie pushed aside the curtains in front of the balcony door and opened it. She stepped outside and surveyed the verdant expanse. "The question is what can we do to help her. It doesn't really matter if it's Drae, a Seventh Order dead-ender, or even a bounty's family member who holds a grudge. The result is the same. Alison's in jail for murder."

Luke shrugged. "Other than making sure the PDA gets here sooner rather than later, there's not much we can do. It's not like the police will share all their evidence with the suspect's friends. Maybe I should return to Washington."

She shook her head. "We might need your help here if something happens."

Mason walked over to the balcony. "I'm half-tempted to go back to Seattle and recruit Drysi and Hana for backup. How quickly do you think it'll take the PDA and FBI to arrive?"

"That depends on the local authorities," the other man replied. "Especially since this is a kemana and the crime's a basic murder. I'd suspect it'll take a minimum of a few days to get them involved, maybe longer. If the police here weren't so understaffed, the feds probably wouldn't even be involved."

He grunted. "We can't sit around here for a week waiting for the PDA. We need to get this—"

A massive explosion erupted from the center of the garden. The shockwave pounded into the side of the resort, shook the entire building, and shattered windows. The force hurled both Mason and Izzie off their feet.

"Shit," she shouted. She groaned and sat up, blood trickling from her forehead. "Did someone actually fire a missile at this place?"

Luke rushed to her side, concern on his face. "Are you okay?"

"I'm fine. It looks worse than it is." She touched her forehead gingerly.

Mason pushed to his feet. He stormed over to the coffee table and yanked his wand up. A massive cloud of dirt and smoke hung in the air, obscuring his fourth-floor view of the garden below him. He raised his wand to cast a shield spell, followed by a speed and strength spell before he narrowed his eyes and crossed the room to focus on the view outside.

The smoke gradually began to clear to reveal the blackened and cracked surface below where a new, deeper crater swallowed the murder site. Trees, shrubs, and flowers surrounding the crater began to crack and tear and their fragments spun into pulsating dust devils. Massive magical pressure emanated from the garden and churned his stomach.

The debris whirled together inside the dust devils. First, a core formed. Larger chunks collided together until lumpy, four-legged creatures with thrashing tendrils stood there. The color of the garden faded to be replaced by the brown and black of the soil as more and more plants gave their lives to form monsters. Most were the size of a large dog, but a few greater threats formed as well, including one creature bigger than Alison's Fiat.

The plant monsters' tendrils thrashed and the tips glowed with diffuse light. Loud pops and cracks sounded as they struck the earth and soil erupted skywards. Mason didn't want to see what the tendrils could do to a person.

He pointed his wand at the rapidly forming horde. "I'm beginning to think I have an idea why they might have wanted Alison out of the way. But at least we have the high ground."

Izzie raised her arms. "Luke, I think you should go to the station and get Alison. I think it's time to say screw the legal consequences. We'll definitely need the help."

The horde continued to grow. A conservative estimate put the enemy number at already over a hundred.

The shifter growled. "And you intend to stay here?"

Strands of light flowed around her and her eyes began to glow. "Yes. I think I'll have to dig deep."

The eyeless plant monsters shuffled toward the resort while their tendrils writhed and twitched ominously.

Several fireballs, colored bolts, and other elemental attacks streaked across the ground and struck the front line. Mason couldn't see the source from his angle, but he assumed some of the hotel security had responded to the explosion. Charred and torn creatures collapsed into piles of vegetable matter, but the efforts barely dented the massive horde's advance ranks.

"Go, Luke," Izzie shouted and ribbons of energy now crackled around her. "If this is Drae, I want to show the Drow bitch what a Jasper Elf can do."

Mason continued to chant. A glowing circle of bright light appeared. Another smaller one appeared lined up with the first. He gritted his teeth as his wand heated.

The security team's assault continued, but it didn't help that for every enemy they felled, a replacement formed. Acres of plant life were twisted and repurposed as an army. Several of the larger monsters now approached, and the security team didn't have the necessary firepower to hold them off.

Luke took a final look at the battle, his expression grim. "I'll be back soon with Alison." He raced out of the room.

Five nested circles now floated in front of Mason's wand. He finished his chant. The rings collapsed on one another and broke into scores of bright, pulsating chunks. They streaked forward, spread out, and detonated along the enemy line to incinerate several creatures outright and shatter a few of the larger ones.

He braced himself on the balcony railing, his heart racing and his breathing ragged. "That's not something I can exactly rapid fire."

Izzie was barely visible in the bright nimbus that surrounded her. A dark cloud grew from a tiny speck over the garden over several seconds until its gloomy expanse covered the entire area. Blue-white light flashed inside.

Lightning blasted from the cloud and obliterated several invaders. Bolt after bolt fell in quick succession, the light blinding and the deafening thunder echoing. The assault was over in thirty seconds, but that was enough.

There was no more plant army, merely blackened earth and smoldering wood, stems, and leaves.

Mason gaped in astonishment. "You can give Alison a run for her money, even when she really gets going."

She fell to her hands and knees, her body covered in sweat and her eyes half-closed. "I'll need a little rest."

He pushed off the railing. "I think that was enough. I don't see any new ones forming."

A tremor shook the building. Dirt and rock began to drift from the crater.

"Or maybe not. Damn it."

The elf took several deep breaths and managed to sit. "This vacation is really starting to suck."

Mason snorted. "Tell me about it. Next time, I'll take Alison to Mount Rushmore."

"With your luck, the presidential heads would grow bodies and attack you."

"Probably." He snickered.

CHAPTER NINETEEN

"What the hell is happening over there?" Alison shouted.

Explosions sounded in the distance and between that and the rapid-fire lightning, it sounded like a war.

Was I wrong? Does Drae not care about the political implications? Or is it not Drae at all? It could be her, and she's finally realizing that Mason, Luke, and Izzie aren't easy prey.

Constable Iritrin sat at a desk and his hands shook. "There are still constables at the resort. They'll handle it. You don't need to worry about it, Brownstone." His voice quivered at the end. "You should worry about yourself. Whatever's happening there doesn't mean anything. You're still on the hook for murder."

She rolled her eyes. "You don't think all that noise might have a little to do with a murder out of nowhere? I'm telling you, the real murderer is on the move again."

"That's a lie. You're the murderer. M-my spell proved it."

"Come on." She kicked the bars and winced. They were

harder than she expected. "I don't know what the hell was up with your spell, but I didn't murder anyone. I was framed and the real murderer is now doing something much worse—maybe even killing many more people."

"Y-you don't know that." He drew his wand but his hand shook so badly that it fell to the desk and rolled. He snatched it up quickly. "It's simply a lie to deflect your own guilt. You're nothing but a rich little princess and who thinks you're better than some mere kemana constable. Maybe you think you can get away with murder, but you're not better than me, Brownstone." He sucked in a few quick breaths. "Because you're in there and I'm out here."

What the hell is this guy's problem?

Alison pounded on the bars. "A Drow princess might be attacking my friends right now. I don't care if you want to lock me up again, but you need to let me out so I can help them. This isn't about being better than you. This is about the fact that I can go toe-to-toe with a Drow princess and you can't. If you want people to die, keep me in here. But if you want to help save people, let me out."

"If this is caused by a Drow princess, the last thing I should do is let another one out to cause trouble," the constable snapped. "Y-you'll stay where you are, Brownstone. If I let you out, half the kemana will burn to the ground."

The door flew open and another officer rushed in, his face red. He rushed over to the desk and grasped the end as he gasped for air.

"The hotel's under attack," he wheezed.

"Attack?" Constable Iritrin swallowed. "Like t-terrorists?"

"An army of magically summoned monsters," the other man explained. "Some guests responded with heavy-duty spells, but reinforcements appeared and they're tougher."

Guests? It sounds like Izzie decided to show them a thing or two.

"Reinforcements?" her guard echoed. "Can't they destroy those too?"

"I don't know." The man shrugged. "There hasn't been a second attack against the army as powerful as the first. The staff is preparing to evacuate the resort."

Alison sighed. "Damn it. I should never have let you bring me in."

The new arrival glanced at her before he looked at his colleague. "We might need to evacuate the entire kemana. The damned creatures are being made out of the material nearby. Resort security's trying to hold the line. They set up barriers, but those turned into monsters, too. We can't fight the entire kemana. We couldn't even if we had fifty constables."

Constable Iritrin stared straight ahead. "No. This can't be happening. This doesn't make sense."

"It damned well is happening, so get it together," the other man shouted. "The others are helping security fight the attackers. We can't sit here. We need to help secure the portal in the resort for the evacuation."

"Whoever ambushed me in town and framed me is responsible," Alison stated clearly. "It's the same person. We were attacked by creatures made from the local environment."

The more I think about it, the more that doesn't sound like a typical Drow spell, but I can think about that later.

"That doesn't change the fact that you were caught lying about a murder," Iritrin replied. "A lying murderer can't be trusted." He managed to stand but his knees joined his hands in shaking. He pointed his wand at the cell, not that an attack would mean much given the warding. "How do we know you're not responsible for this, Brownstone? Maybe you planned to get arrested so you could have an alibi when the worse crime occurred. Isn't it mighty convenient? If people get hurt, maybe you should, too."

Take a vacation, Alison, they said. It'll be relaxing, they said. At this rate, if I try to go on my honeymoon, World War III will start.

She folded her arms, too annoyed to be afraid. "Are you serious right now? You're threatening the one woman who can help you."

The other constable placed his arm on his shoulder. "Her friends are still in the resort. I don't know what happened with the murder, but I doubt she has anything to do with what's going on now."

"Maybe they're the ones doing it." He shrugged the arm off angrily. "We never had any serious trouble here until she came. Now, we have brutal murders and monster hordes. It's all her fault." Flecks of spittle joined the increased volume of his last sentence. "The arrogant bitch thinks we're toys she can play with."

"That's ridiculous." She made no effort to hide her scorn. "I've dedicated my career to protecting people. If I wanted to hurt innocent people, why bother stopping the Fremont Troll? Or the Seventh Order? Or any of the bounties I've apprehended? I don't know what crawled up your ass, Constable. Do you want me to say it's my fault?" She threw her hands up. "Maybe it is. Maybe someone targeted this place because of me. I don't know, but I do know I could be out there helping right now."

Several loud explosions thundered outside. They weren't that far from the hotel, only a few minutes by foot. If the monsters overran the resort, they would be at the police station soon after.

Luke rushed into the station. The two constables pointed their wands at him.

He growled. "Don't point those sticks at me if you don't want me to break your fingers. I'm not in the damned mood." He nodded at the cell. "And let her out. We need her help."

Constable Iritrin uttered a strangled laugh. "You can't order us around, shifter. This isn't DC."

"I don't have time for your bullshit, asshole." Luke looked at Alison. "I think Izzie threw something major. She was charging to fire at the horde when I left, but I'm also worried she might have overextended herself."

Alison gritted her teeth and tried to force magic to form a shadow blade, but the magic simply dissipated. She tried to twist streams of shadow magic more tightly together, weaving and overlapping them. With a yell, she managed to shunt more energy into her hand. The outline of a blade began to form.

I've never been able to shadow compress so well.

Constable Iritrin spun toward the cell, his eyes wide. "What are you doing?"

She locked eyes with him and held the nebulous form of the half-formed blade for a few seconds before she released the energy.

"That's right," the constable sputtered. "J-just because you could manage half a spell doesn't mean anything. You can't break out of that cell. It could hold Rhazdon in her prime."

"Listen, you stupid asshole," she shouted. "I did it as a demonstration to show you how much power I have. Right now, my friends, the security team, and your fellow cops are out there fighting an army of monsters. I don't know if a Drow princess is responsible, but you have one in a cell who is pissy and ready to kick ass, so why don't you let me out so I can direct that rage where it will be useful?"

Great. I've turned into Dad. All I need is a whiny, blood-thirsty amulet.

Luke stormed over to the officer and hoisted the wizard by the lapels, his eyes yellow. "Do you think she's a killer? Then let her kill." He threw him down and glared at the other constable, but the man shook his head and backed away.

"Nothing like this is supposed to happen here," Iritrin murmured. "This is supposed to be a safe place. It's not my fault. It's Brownstone's fault. It has to be. It all started when she came."

The other man retrieved a large silver key from his pocket. "I'll take responsibility for letting her out. If Brownstone did kill someone, maybe she had a reason and she couldn't tell us, but he's right. We need her right now."

"You can't let her out!" his colleague shouted. His wand lay on the ground now, his hand on top of it. "Everything will be ruined if you let her out."

"No, it won't. Sometimes, you need a monster to fight a monster."

Alison rolled her eyes. "I'm not a monster or a murderer but whatever. Get me out of here before my friends are beaten to death by a real monster."

He walked toward the cell with a determined look, the key ready in his hand.

Constable Iritrin bounded to his feet and pointed his wand at his colleague. "We'll be fine," he seethed. "You will not let her out."

The other man stared at the wand. "What are you doing?"

"Stopping you from making a mistake." Iritrin sighed, the panic gone from his face. Resignation had replaced it. "No matter what, you won't let Alison Brownstone out of that cell."

"Haven't you listened to anything I've said? We need to protect everyone. Even if we open the portal, it means we'll have to defend it and we can use her."

"No," he shouted. "They promised me we would be fine as long as we kept her in the cell. If I break the deal, who knows what they might do? This is the safer way for everyone. I won't risk other people's lives."

"What?" The other cop narrowed her eyes. "Who are you talking about? What deal?"

Luke growled. "You son of a bitch. You set Alison up. Are you the murderer?"

"I didn't murder anyone." Iritrin jerked the wand at first one man, then the other. "No one's dead. There wasn't a murder at all, only a conjured doll that was destroyed." He uttered a panicked laugh. "I only needed a day or two more. I could have left and the FBI and PDA would never have found me. No one will get hurt. No one's been hurt."

Alison scoffed. "Those monsters attacking might disagree."

"They won't go any farther than the resort. People will be evacuated. It'll be fine."

"You betrayed the kemana," she hissed. "You're a cop. You're supposed to protect people. What is this? Terrorist bullshit? Are you from a dark wizard family?"

"Dark wizards? They're even more pompous than you." He laughed. "Screw you, Brownstone. You're like the rest. All you guests are nothing more than pampered rich degenerates who come here because your busy lives of wealth and luxury are too exhausting. I'm tired of watching over a dying town while you sit there and sip on wine and eat caviar."

"So you took a bribe to sell out the resort and the kemana?" She smirked. "And here I had this complicated scenario worked out involving illusions, shapeshifting, and special magic. It's like I told a woman a few days ago. Sometimes, it's easier to not use magic."

"Put the wand down, Iritrin." The other constable shook his head. "If you surrender, this doesn't have to go badly for you. I'll make sure everyone knows you cooperated."

A new series of loud explosions shook the building.

The traitor licked his lips and his gaze darted around the room. "We can split the money. Come with me now. We kill the shifter and Brownstone. She's in the cell and will be easy to take out."

"No. Put your wand down."

"Put that damned key down now, or I will fucking kill you!"

Luke snorted. "I've had enough of this crap." He leapt toward Iritrin. The constable tried a quick chant, but the shifter's fist found his jaw first. His head snapped back and he collapsed with a loud thud and Luke kicked his wand away. "Get her out of there."

The other man shoved the key in the lock and turned. He threw open the door. "Please, Miss Brownstone. I don't know what to say about Iritrin. I'm sorry, but I beg you to help protect the resort and the kemana."

She stepped out of the cell and strode toward the exit. "You don't need to beg me to protect people."

CHAPTER TWENTY

Alison and Luke pushed through the thick crowd surrounding the resort entrance. Smoke billowed from behind the building and spread along the rocky, glowing roof of the kemana.

Guests streamed out of the building and through the crowd. Some headed deeper into town, directed by clusters of resort employees who looked anxious and concerned. Others hurried toward open portals. Each revealed the interiors of different buildings. With all the elite magicals in the building, even if they lacked the combat experience of Alison and her friends, many would have access to high-end spells.

The bellhop helped a limping woman covered with green scales whose several lacerations oozed blue blood. Alison didn't recognize her species.

"We're almost there, ma'am," the Nicht explained as they approached a portal. She glanced at Alison and a glimmer of faint hope appeared in her eyes.

I know. I'm here. I'll do something, and I'll make whoever is responsible pay for what they've done.

"There's no way they'll be able to get everyone out of here quickly," she commented as they entered the lobby. Shouting and crying people filled the area. Most tried to get outside, but others waved and called out for their friends and family.

"The guests, maybe," she continued, "but what about every person in town? If it's bad enough that they need to evacuate, it's bad enough that they can't leave a couple of thousand other people waiting to die."

"Maybe that's the point." Luke growled. "It's not like terrorists haven't destroyed a kemana before. For all we know, they might need a large number of dead people as part of a ritual."

"Dark wizards?" She swallowed. All along, she'd been so convinced she was the target and a Drow princess the aggressor but sometimes, luck could be cruel in a different way. What if her presence was incidental? It didn't matter. For the moment, she needed to stop the attack and protect everyone. Finding someone to blame could come later.

"Seattle and Charlottesville," Luke snapped through gritted teeth. "Who knows where else? This place is power waiting to be tapped, and it's barely hanging on. It makes an excellent target. The PDA even has a program to monitor some of the smaller kemanas because of the potential risk. They simply don't like to talk about it."

An elderly man in a bathrobe fell and cried out in pain. Several people walked past and ignored his groans.

The shifter rushed over to him and helped the man stand. "Go on without me, Alison. I can do more out here than I can there. I'll do what I do best—try to boss people around, convinced that I'm actually helping them."

She lingered for a moment before she nodded and ran into the hallway leading to the back. Once there, she summoned a shield and wings, rose to the ceiling, and accelerated over a few rushing stragglers on her way toward the garden. Only a few people spared her the briefest of glances as they fled.

After a few quick turns, she emerged into the open. A line of security and constables crouched behind slanted metal shields and fired spells at the large, dark shadows outlined in the thick smoke that smothered the area. One wizard lay pale and unconscious on the ground. Sebastian lay on his back, a deep gouge through his chest, which no longer rose and fell, his eyes open in a death stare.

Damn. What a waste.

The garden itself had been turned into a burning wasteland. Craters filled the area, along with the smoldering and broken remains of the conjured monsters—piles of wood, rock, metal, and even fabric. A headless dirt giant emerged from the smoke and raised its thick, rock-fingered arms. They glowed with a dull light. Several smaller four-legged rock creatures skittered around the legs of the massive figure.

The explosions and battle had decimated the garden, but most of the nearby buildings had been spared, with only a few smaller gazebos and storage sheds destroyed. Some of the exterior of the hotel wings had been scorched, but much it remained untouched.

Dirt blasted away from the body as the wizards pelted the monster and its retinue with a colorful array of spells.

A dense black metal lance hurtled from one wizard. A black square so dark it seemed to eat the light tumbled through the air and ripped through the giant. Several other attacks erupted from balconies at different angles and struck the shadows in the cloud.

So, it's not only Izzie and Mason helping, huh? I have to hand it to these security guys. They didn't cut and run. They have already saved dozens if not hundreds of lives.

Alison was reminded of the attack on the School of Necessary Magic. Attacking any place filled with magicals always brought a risk, even if they weren't combat-trained.

A bright white light flashed above and a huge crackling sphere screamed from several stories up and separated into several smaller ones. They exploded along the ground like a cluster bomb to rend the ground and incinerate several of the aggressors.

That must be Izzie.

A constable looked at Alison. "They keep coming. While they aren't hard to kill, they're endless. It's like we're fighting the entire garden itself, down to the rocks." He pointed to a pile of twisted metal a few yards away. "Anything we make that's too far forward becomes them. And the materials don't react to normal manipulation spells, only significant damage. The only thing we have going for us is they seem focused on us as long as we keep attacking them. They're trying to rush out in different directions."

She nodded and could only imagine the carnage that would have occurred. A small security team and a handful of cops, even with magic, wouldn't have been enough. Even Izzie and Alison would haven't been able to stop a truly wild army.

The latest giant and its allies finally subsided into piles of dirt and rock, but several more creatures emerged from the smoke.

Her expression grim, she planted her feet and channeled energy between her hands to feed a bright blue-white sphere. She finished charging and flung the spell and the resulting detonation obliterated a half-metal giant that advanced on the defensive line.

"There has to be something or someone that created them," she stated. "If they're being made out of everything, you were right before. There's no way we'll win."

The constable shrugged before he struck a tiny metal man with a fireball. "There was an explosion. We rushed out here and there were already a ton of monsters. One of the guests above annihilated a horde of them, but they kept coming."

Thanks, Izzie. You probably saved this place from getting overrun.

"I'll do my best to help," Alison replied. "But we need to find the source."

"Thanks, but I don't even know if it matters at this point. We can barely hold them here, let alone try to move forward. We only need to hold long enough to evacuate the guests."

"Understood. I have some ideas."

"If it ends this fight, then go for it," the constable said, his tone stark.

Alison threw a few hasty light bolts. She felled a few smaller creatures before she elevated and headed toward her balcony, which she approached from the side.

Mason and Izzie, pale and bathed in sweat, both leaned over the railing, their breathing ragged.

She slowed and hovered a few feet away from the balcony railing. "Do you know where these things are coming from? The guys on the ground don't have a clue, and I don't like how either you or they are looking."

"It has to be centered around where the murder was," Mason replied. "That's where all this started. It was easier to tell before everyone began to explode things, including us." He cast a quick fireball and his attack cut through the smoke before it removed an arm from an advancing dirt giant.

"There was no murder, but we can talk about that later." She bit her lip, concerned because she'd not seen Izzie so spent in a long time. "Even your power isn't unlimited, Izzie. If I'm right, you already did your part."

"Yes, I kind of screwed up." She managed a weak grin. "It's because I had to start out with a big spell, but at least these new waves are slower so I bought people time, but I'm not out of juice yet."

"This is endless, A," he complained. "And they're getting steadily bigger even if they are getting slower. I don't think we can hold them here. We need to end this game of whack-a-mole and destroy the source."

Alison sighed. "That's what they said down there."

"Maybe containment?"

"The only way we'd be able to do it is with a wall, and they'll simply convert that. Even Izzie and I don't have the power to sustain a purely magical field big enough to seal off an army."

She peered into the smoke, raised her hand to her face,

and murmured a spell. The shimmer intensified around her head. She'd now be able to breathe even surrounded by heavy smoke. "Okay, then. I'll end it. I'll find the source. Let's hope I don't get killed by everyone else's attacks."

"A," Mason whispered. "Be careful."

Alison grinned. "Careful might get us all killed."

"You still owe me a marriage."

"I'll keep that in mind." She smiled, plunged into the smoke, and strafed a rock giant with a barrage of light bolts. Her shields muted the heat in the air around her as she descended toward the fake murder site. Even without the obscuring smoke, the blasted hellscape lacked even a hint of the original garden's layout, which forced her to slow and reorient herself.

There were no obvious artifacts bright with power and no dark wizards chanting in long-forgotten languages.

Damn it. Cut me break here.

New monsters continued to form all over the garden, both giant and small, but now that she was farther into the battlefield, something felt off. The intense magical pressure dominating the area felt uneven like it pooled in the garden but didn't emanate from there. She would need to go even lower.

Is Luke right? Is this dark wizards? Shit. For all, I know the Tapestry figured out how to come back. If this is Drae, though, she doesn't get to laugh this off. She's dead, and I don't care what that means to Drow politics. No one can put thousands of peoples' lives at risk and walk away like it didn't happen.

She settled on her feet in the center of a deep crater. A massive ice lance pounded into a rock giant that stood on the lip and hurled the creature back. It plummeted and landed with a loud crash. Barely visible in the dark smoke, the monster began to stand, but her light bolt blasts severed its limbs. The body fell again and reverted to being nothing more dangerous than an inanimate pile of rocks.

With a few quick motions with her hands, she chanted a new spell. A summoned wind whipped past her to cool the air and blow some of the smoke away. Being able to breathe and tolerate the heat was useless if she couldn't find the clue she needed, though.

There has to be something—a glyph, an artifact, a wizard, even a freaking Overseer or Mountain Strider. There's no way someone enchanted this whole area to spew monsters. If someone was that powerful and they wanted to hurt people, they would simply nuke the entire resort and not bother with something so elaborate.

Several smaller creatures formed from the exposed bedrock. She wasn't sure if there was a problem with the spell or if they were purposefully supposed to be nothing more than two glowing razor-claw-tipped arms attached to a rough chest shape.

What are these? Like half a body? Rock half-zombies?

The monsters whipped their arms to fling themselves at her. She destroyed two in mid-leap. A third scratched at her and its claws strained her shields. It landed and continued to hack at her legs.

Alison extended a shadow blade and sliced the creature in half. She spun toward loud overlapping scratching noises behind her in time to see a half-dozen of the creatures soar toward her. They thudded on and around her, swarmed her, and their limbs sliced and ripped with an intensity that surprised her. She hissed when one penetrated her shield and gashed her side. Ignoring the sharp pain, she shook them off and eliminated them with a flurry of stabs and cuts.

This is starting to get really, really annoying. How do you win a fight against acres and acres of land?

Her side throbbed and she layered more shields. Given how they had pierced her defenses, the little slicing bastards must have possessed some anti-magic ability in those claws. That made her wonder about all the monsters. Sebastian might have been surprised by that fact and ended up dead.

This can't be Drae. This goes beyond a Drow being feisty in an act of war. This doesn't accomplish what she wants. It doesn't push me away from caring. It only pisses me off, and if she doesn't want me involved, riling me up is the last thing she'd want to do.

A few fireballs screamed into the crater from above and exploded to throw up rock and dust.

It's not only Mason and Izzie up there, and maybe not everyone has seen me. I have to hurry.

Another group of slicers formed out of the rock and launched themselves at her. She elevated hastily to avoid the swarm and hovered a few yards above the crater. They landed in an untidy heap and jumped at her, their angry claws outstretched like rabid beasts desperate for her flesh.

She took a deep breath and pushed shadow magic into a stream. When she had enough, she twisted and concentrated the magical energy before she eased it into her wounded side. Shadows swallowed the wound and the pain faded.

That was much better than I've been able to do before. At least I'm getting some decent practice here.

The continued cacophony and flashes behind her reminded her that the fight wasn't over simply because she could avoid a few enemies. She needed to find the source before the monsters overwhelmed the defenders or Sebastian wouldn't be the only casualty. Anti-magic claws could kill many people who might otherwise think they were safe.

Come on, Alison. Think. There has to be something you've missed.

As she tried to focus, she took a deep breath and her air filter and spells prevented her from breathing in a lungful of anything but warm air. Monsters lumbered forward on either side of the crater while their smaller kin crawled, skittered, or bounded forward. Other than the pile of slicers, none of the creatures paid her any attention.

Am I not close enough?

Alison narrowed her eyes. The smoke had begun to creep in and fill the hole left by her wind spell. Only the swarming clawed aberrations appeared to come directly from the crater, but the others didn't seem to come from directly behind it either. There was a noticeable gap in the advancing horde. The creatures didn't walk to the back edge and circle around. They joined the flow on either side from farther back.

Why? Are they afraid of falling in?

She drifted from one side of the crater to another and tried to ignore the chaos around her and the growing slicer army beneath her while she concentrated. The magical pressure was the key. There were differences in what she could sense. The heavy level of magic made them hard to discern, but subtle differences remained. She doubted she would have been able to feel them without exploring the crater.

Her new awareness prompted her to increase her altitude and she flew deeper into the gardens. She passed over newly forming monsters. The smoke grew blindingly thick before she emerged into an area of actual green and color —living plants. The end of the grounds lay farther beyond and the surface grew rocky. Something flickered in the distance.

There we go. Now I've got you.

CHAPTER TWENTY-ONE

A burst of speed enabled her to quickly close the gap between her and the mysterious flicker. The garden disappeared and gave way to dusty, rocky ground and stony outcroppings. Cavern walls loomed on several sides, reminding her that despite the size of the area, she was still underground. She slowed and frowned as the source of the flicker came more clearly into view—a familiar woman but now in a red robe covered with runes and surrounded by a bright yellow light that pulsed and flickered.

Of all the people I had to run into, it's her?

"Jade," she declared. "I want to believe you aren't Drae but now, I don't know what to think."

"Drae?" the woman echoed, her face pinched in confusion. "I don't know who that is, so I'm reasonably sure I'm not her." She clucked her tongue. "You need to take a good, hard look at your life, Alison, if there are so many different people who are such dangerous threats."

"Trust me. I think that all that time, but you can't protect people without making a few dangerous enemies."

She landed and pointed her shadow blade at the other woman. "Drae's a Drow princess. I've been half-convinced this entire time it was her, but all this..." She gestured to the smoke and fire in the distance. "All this chaos is too much."

"This Drae sounds like she's not willing to do what it takes for her goals. I pity her, then."

"And you are willing?" she asked.

"Obviously." Jade shrugged. "I wouldn't have put in all this time and effort if I wasn't. It took months of planning and weeks of actual preparation. I'll say this for you, Alison. Whatever flaws you may have, when it's time to do what is needed, you do it. That's admirable. You might hate me now, but I do think you're a strong, impressive woman worthy of respect."

"I'm glad you feel that way. Maybe then you'll listen when I say you should stop this now before more people are hurt. People have already died—and I mean real people, not fake victims."

"So you worked that out, did you? That might explain why they let you go so quickly. I underestimated you. You aren't renowned for your diplomatic abilities, so I thought my little scheme would have occupied you for far longer."

"I don't care," she replied. "But I do care about the people who are in danger. You can end this. I've found you and I'm willing to show you mercy if you do the right thing."

Jade stared at the smoke and flames in the distance. "Say please."

Alison shrugged. "Please stop this. I beg you to stop it." She didn't mind a little humility if it saved people's lives.

"It was a good effort." The woman shook her head. "But I'm afraid I can't do that, Alison."

"I can't even take a vacation without something happening," she muttered and strode forward. "If you won't surrender, I'll have to stop you, and it won't be pleasant for you." A few yards away from her adversary, an invisible force pounded into her and she careened back. She landed hard with a grunt and rolled, her shields weakened and her head swimming.

"This is the glory of what normal humans can accomplish when they put their mind to it," her attacker declared. "With a few minor tweaks and amplifiers, I've turned a few artifacts into something that even the great Dark Princess can't stop." She rolled one of her sleeves to reveal long silver strips on her skin. "To be fair, this whole plan relies on technology that is the product of billions of dollars and decades of research. The artifacts alone are probably worth billions." She laughed. "I could have sold them and lived a life of luxury. It's almost a shame that I didn't leave them to be found, but I had to save it from the government. They're so twisted about magic, there was a good chance they might have destroyed them. Think about that. Knowledge eliminated to maintain a false balance."

"Who are you?" she demanded. "Why are you doing this?"

"I'm doing this to prove a point," Jade declared and her face twitched into a scowl. "To prove to the world how dangerous magic is. To prove to even magicals how dangerous it is." She gestured to the resort in the distance. "This palace of privilege where elite magicals can relax— and one woman can cause havoc."

Alison wasn't sure billions of dollars and decades of research counted as one woman spreading havoc, but she wasn't there to debate her, only stop her.

"You're New Veil?" she demanded, her voice quaking with hatred.

The woman shuddered and looked insulted. "I'm not one of those psychopaths. They're merely killers who are looking for an excuse. I'm a scholar, a scientist. I'm a woman who has dedicated her life to making the world better for people." She pointed to her face. "The babyface helps. I look much younger than I am. It throws people off like it threw you off." She smirked. "I'm not even from Nebraska, by the way."

What the hell was in that barrier?

"If this is about punishing me, leave everyone else out of it." She shook her head. For some reason, she still had trouble concentrating and her vision was blurry. She took a few deep breaths. "People don't deserve to die because you have a vendetta against me."

Jade scoffed. "Don't be so arrogant. Not everything's about you."

"You could have fooled me with all the framing me for drunken incidents and murder."

"Your presence here was a great bonus and allowed me to have a little fun. You can call that petty revenge if you want, but it's justified." She sneered. "I intended for you to sit helplessly while this place was destroyed, but not all plans work out. It's a shame in a sense. I don't truly want to kill you, but now, you've left me no choice."

"I don't even know who you are," Alison pointed out. "I

understand that I'm not the main target here, but why do you want revenge against me?"

"Because you destroyed a great man. You are personally responsible for stalling technomagic research because of your own selfish concerns." Jade glared at her. "It's one of the reasons I find you such a disappointment. I admired you as much as I admired him."

"What are you talking about?" She gasped when she recalled their first conversation. "You're talking about Scott Carlyle, aren't you?"

"Yes," Jade all but snarled, her face vicious with rage. "Scott Carlyle will die before he leaves prison. People act like he's a monster, but all he did was see the future and make a few select sacrifices. He would have made sure that magicals and non-magicals could have lived together in peace, but that wasn't good enough for you. Instead, you craved more power."

She rolled her eyes. "Excuse me if I don't trust the plans of a man who used genetically engineered magical viruses on innocent people. He lied to people and he murdered people."

"Are you so much better?" the woman shouted. "You kill people all the time. Scott's actions could have saved millions—maybe billions—and now, a war is inevitable."

"Spare me the painful justification of evil speech. The man was out of control. He even used his own people to feed his technomagic armor at the end." Her face twisted in disgust. "I would never sacrifice other people to save myself. He's lucky I didn't kill him right then and there. That in itself proves he was an asshole, Jade."

"That isn't my real name of course," the woman

explained. "But I needed to disappear after you destroyed my boss. I was a researcher for Advanced Magitek Systems for my entire career, but I didn't have the honor of working on the virus project."

"How sad for you. How did you ever sleep at night?"

Jade's mouth twitched. "You're seeing the fruits of my specialty—technomagical magical enhancement. I managed to escape the FBI and PDA because I was away on an artifact collection project at the time. Even then, the dig site was raided, but I was the only one to escape. It's almost like fate did its best to protect me and bring me to this moment."

The clouds in Alison's head began to part. "You think fate led you to attack this resort? And you have the gall to call me arrogant?"

Okay, I can't get close, but that doesn't mean she's immune to spells. If she were, she wouldn't hide all the way back here.

"This whole place proves everything Scott claimed." Jade's glow brightened for a moment. "The kemana is the ultimate expression of the separation of magicals from non-magicals. The local police are supposed to be trust-worthy and uphold the law, but I didn't even need a sophisticated artifact to manipulate him, only a simple bribe. Bribe a normal human and there's only so much he can do, but corruptible magicals are, by their very nature, exponentially more dangerous."

"That's one man," Alison countered. "The others have risked their lives to hold your monsters off. They could have easily run, but they didn't. They're doing their best to protect others. If you think you can indict all magicals because of the actions of one corrupt man, I have all of non-magical history to point to."

"Yes, the other police." Jade frowned. "I didn't expect them to let you out so quickly. When I saw you, I was excited. I wanted to toy with and test you, but part of me wondered if I would risk my mission by doing so. At the end, I suppose my instincts proved right. I think I let my admiration get in the way of what needed to be done. I should have killed you when you weren't expecting it."

"That's harder than you think. Trust me. Many people have tried." She took a few steps back and raised her palm. "Surrender. You've already killed at least one person, so I'll do you a favor by offering you a chance to give up."

The woman shook her head. "You didn't make the world safer by destroying my boss. You made the world more dangerous. All I'm doing is making that clear. This isn't meant to be sadistic and I'm sorry that people have already died, but I should point out that if I only wanted to kill people, there are different ways I could have gone about it. I'm not a terrorist. I'm an educator."

"Turn your damned artifacts off," she shouted. "I don't want to have to kill you, but I'll do what I have to do to save people. This is your last chance."

"I knew there was a good chance I wouldn't leave this resort alive." Jade drew a wavy blade Alison recognized as a kris from her robe. "It's too late, Alison. But don't worry. My army is almost out of power."

Her breath caught. "Then it's all over?"

"It doesn't matter because I've made my point. I entertained thoughts of escape, but now that you're here, I might as well complete Scott's revenge."

"Meaning what?" Bile rose in the back of her throat. A self-destruct artifact?

If I shield myself enough, I can survive, but I'd need her to detonate here so no one else gets hurt.

Jade's smile had a regretful quality to it. "You win, in a sense. I won't use the last of my power to fuel the army." She revealed a small slab of stone covered in worn and barely visible Futhark runes. "This was always the key to my plan. I was lucky to find it on that dig before I went on the run. A summoning artifact of great power."

Alison released a sigh of relief and lowered her arm. "Then it's over. You can put the knife down."

"You don't understand. The new creations will stop forming soon. It's only my enhancement devices combined with the latent energy of the kemana that have allowed the artifacts to function as long as they have." She held the kris in front of her. "But I still have this."

"I thought you were giving up."

"No. I'm giving my life as a sacrifice."

"Stop!"

"This will be the instrument of my revenge and the ultimate expression of my research." Jade plunged the knife into her heart and fell to her knees.

Alison's eyes widened. "What the hell?"

Blood seeped from her mouth. "You lose, Alison Brownstone. I give my life to make my final point."

"Killing yourself doesn't mean you win. You won't be remembered as anything but a maniac. Even Scott Carlyle didn't kill himself in the end."

"He needs to live. I'm merely a tool of his vision." Jade fell forward and her whole body trembled. Her face twisted in pain as she forced out the words, determined to have the last say. "And you still don't understand, but you will. I'm simply proving something we've long since learned when it comes to magic and myth— many are truer than we ever knew. I couldn't call him without a sacrifice."

A huge tremor shook the area. Rock ripped from the ground and nearby outcroppings in a swirling maelstrom. Small pieces pounded together and fused in a bright flash. Even pieces of the roof of the massive cavern flew toward the rapidly glowing stone cyclone. The outline of a titanic body began to form. Alison backed away as the creature took shape. The ground stopped shaking as the last pieces joined together.

A gargantuan eight-legged gray stone horse towered over her. The monstrous new creation could have stamped on the earlier giants and looked like it could leap over the resort with ease. Dull red light illuminated its eyes and arcs of black energy crackled over its body.

"I give you my version of Sleipnir," Jade wheezed. "I win." Her head slumped and she stopped breathing.

Alison strengthened her shields and wings and rose quickly. "Sure, what's a vacation without an angry giant eight-legged horse?"

CHAPTER TWENTY-TWO

Her heart in her throat, Alison circled Sleipnir in search of something that looked like a weakness. The gray stone seemed to go on forever, and there was no obvious glowing heart or cracks, merely a massive eight-legged stone horse. She hissed when a crack of dark lightning strained her shield.

His bellow shook the entire area.

I can't let him anywhere near town, which means I need to keep his attention.

She took a few deep breaths before she surged over his back and launched a few bolts of light magic. They exploded against the surface of the monster and while they scorched the body, they didn't loosen anything or even make a dent. Another earthshaking bellow followed, and the animal turned. His steps left deep prints in the rocky ground. When he snapped at her, she spun to the side and narrowly avoided being bitten in half. Even with her shields, she didn't want to risk a direct strike.

Is it like the other monsters? Is it merely an animated version of the material? I can chip away at it maybe.

Her initial attacks alternated between shadow crescents and light blasts as she trailed along the side like a gnat trying to fight a horse. Her strafing run left a trail of explosions but little real damage. The monster roared in anger. At least she'd annoyed him.

Sleipnir whirled and reared. Four of his legs kicked into the air. A quick turn saved her from one leg, but the hoof of another clipped her. Black lightning blasted over her and ripped through her shields. She careened toward the wall and an acrid stench filled her nose. At a safer distance, she leveled her flight and hovered in place with a hiss as pain seared from burns in her back.

That wasn't fun, and now I know it's not only about hitting hard.

She tossed a few rapid light bolts his way to draw his attention.

Sleipnir rounded on her and roared. She tried to not question her decision. Black lightning bolts launched in several directions and blasted into the ground, roof, and cavern walls. Each strike gouged the area and left a jagged, dark scar.

"At least I have his attention," she muttered as she regenerated her shields and sealed her wounds. Fatigue sapped at her, but she was far from spent. She merely needed to identify the best strategy. There was no such thing as an enemy without a weakness.

She glanced at the resort. The smoke wasn't as dense as before, and she couldn't make out any large moving shapes.

Did they win? Or is there merely a temporary lull? It won't matter if I don't destroy this thing.

Izzie's help against Sleipnir might have been nice but given the kinds of spells she had already mustered, she would probably barely be able to stand. Too many people didn't understand that being a powerful magical wasn't the same thing as having unlimited power, even for a powerful Jasper Elf like Izzie.

Another barrage of black lightning shredded the surroundings. One blast struck near Jade and hurled her body a few feet away.

What a damned waste. This woman collected all those artifacts and used all that research for this plan. She could have added so much to the world, even without magic. I thought Carlyle understood that once, too.

Alison dropped altitude and passed through between Sleipnir's legs. She tossed a couple of explosive orbs at the limbs and managed to knock a few flecks of stone loose. It was progress—not great progress, but at least she had established that he wasn't completely invulnerable. She emerged from beneath the beast and retreated, keeping her distance.

If I can break pieces off, I simply need more power.

He took a ponderous step toward the resort and shook a few more rocks from above. After a few steps, she realized the beast no longer cared about the tiny Drow woman who offered pinprick attacks. She felt a little insulted.

"Shit." She landed on one knee. It was time to go all out, no matter how risky it was. She released her wings and raised her arms. "Hey, you eight-legged asshole. I'm not done with you."

This would all have been far easier if it actually was Drae.

She took several deep breaths and channeled magic into a growing blue-white spinning lance in front of her. The weapon hummed with power and the volume increased with each passing second. She threaded her magic in slowly and deliberately, taking her time with her shadow compression. The lance crackled and dense dark lines continued to spread throughout the length. She kept her breathing steady as she continued to feed it power.

Come on, come on, come on. I can do this. I have to do this. I'm one of the few people here who can.

Her body strained to control the large concentration of magical energy and she gritted her teeth with the effort.

Sleipnir took another few steps forward and she released her attack. The lance rocketed toward its target, a bright missile of light. It struck one of the back legs and exploded. A shower of stone and glowing particles rained from the wound. Massive cracks splintered through the limb and back of the beast. She'd managed to blow off the entire back half of the leg.

Alison yelped in triumph. "Ha! You're not so tough, are you?"

The stone beast turned. His lengthy bellow shook the entire area.

"Pissy much? Then kill me before you go after anyone else. Wait. What?"

Her eyes widened. The wounds on Sleipnir glowed and new stone grew to fill the holes and cracks. Even with the kemana and shadow compression, she wasn't sure she could launch major attacks quickly enough to win.

Damn it.

A bright blast of energy screamed from the resort and punched into her adversary. The latest assault gouged a huge chunk out of his exposed side and he roared in anger.

She grinned.

Thanks, Izzie. I'm glad you still have some juice in you.

Several large fireballs erupted against the beast. They didn't do as much damage as Izzie or Alison's attacks, but Sleipnir hesitated after the impacts and bellowed in defiance. More dark lightning savaged the immediate area but he didn't fire at the resort.

Yeah, now we're talking.

Alison took a few deep breaths and began to charge a new attack. She was certain now that the resort defenders had defeated the last of Jade's lesser forces. Other than Izzie, they might lack Alison's power, but even from miles away it wasn't hard to hit a building-sized monster.

The smaller attacks—fireballs and lightning mostly—came as a staccato assault. They didn't seem to hurt Sleipnir but his earlier wounds had ceased regenerating.

We can do this. We can win. I need to make sure their efforts don't go to waste.

She dropped to one knee and bit her lip as she poured magic into her attack. This time, she intended to blast through the body of the animal, even if she had to draw on every last ounce of magic available to her. He turned fully toward her, stepped forward, and ignored the barrage of attacks on his flanks.

That's right. Come and get me. I won't run. I'll annihilate you instead. I'm Alison fucking Brownstone, and I'm not afraid of stupid giant horses with eight legs.

A bright beam fired from the resort and streaked into

the horse to sever two of his back legs. He roared in pain but his six remaining legs kept him from falling. Cracks now traced up several of his limbs and his body. The latest attack drew his attention away from her, and he turned and exposed his side.

Perfect.

Alison screamed and released her latest attack. Her digging lance missiled toward the cracked center of Sleipnir's body. She squinted when the bright explosion consumed the center. A moment later, a dark shockwave blasted out of the beast as the entire creature blew apart in a secondary explosion.

"Oh, shit," she muttered.

The shockwave struck her. Agony overwhelmed her as she catapulted helplessly and landed with a breath-stealing crunch atop an outcropping. Something was probably broken but she hurt too much everywhere else to know for sure. She groaned as her body rolled down the side of the outcropping and she bounced painfully to level ground.

She fought against the darkness that threatened to overwhelm her consciousness and focused her few strands of consciousness on shadow healing. All she needed to do was not die over the next few minutes.

I guess I need a little work still, she thought as she passed out.

Alison groaned and blinked her eyes open. Her head throbbed but the body-searing agony from before was gone. She sat and realized that she lay on the rubble-strewn ground beside a rock outcropping.

"Why is Mason's t-shirt draped over me?" she asked.

"I wasn't sure if you wanted to wake up naked," he replied from behind her. "And I wasn't sure if anyone else was coming." He shrugged. "Then again, you are known for flying around gardens naked."

"I'm glad to see we can joke when I nearly died." She turned slowly. He stood there shirtless, his well-earned abs on display and his wand in hand. Her breath caught when she reminded herself he was all hers. "What happened?" she murmured.

"We won. After that monster exploded and you didn't fly back, I came looking for you. You weren't as badly off as I expected, but I assumed you wouldn't mind a little healing magic from your life wizard fiancé."

"Izzie?" She held her breath. "Is she okay? She went crazy with those spells toward the end."

"She kind of overdid it, but she's asleep," he reassured her. "I took her to the security team so they could keep an eye on her before I ran here."

She yawned. "I could use sleep, too." Clumsily and a little stiffly, she stood and took a moment to pull the t-shirt on. Only a few scraps remained from her original clothes.

"Was it Drae?" Mason asked. "I assume you found whoever was responsible since the army stopped and that huge-ass horse appeared."

Alison shook her head. "She had nothing to do with it. I'll explain later."

"But it's over?" He wounded worried.

She nodded. "Yeah. It's over." She stared at the resort in

the distance, the lingering smoke and fires a reminder of the intense battle just waged. "Do you know what I need, Mason?"

"What is it, A? I'll get anything you need."

Her grin was teasing. "I need a vacation from my vacation."

CHAPTER TWENTY-THREE

The next afternoon, Alison sipped a glass of wine in one of the bars in the resort. Izzie sat across from her, also with a glass. The only other person in the entire room was a grateful-looking bartender.

The Jasper Elf leaned forward to stare at her friend.

"What is it?" Alison asked. "Is there something on my face?"

Izzie shook her head. "You know, I wasn't sure before, but I am now. You're a little darker."

"I am?"

"Yes. Nothing dramatic, more kind of like a light tan. It looks good on you."

"I am half-Drow." She shrugged. "I'll eventually be fairly dark, I suppose, but I hadn't really noticed. I guess it was too gradual for me and everyone at the company."

"I almost didn't notice myself," her companion admitted. "I had to think about how light you were these last couple of years. It's simply something that came to mind now that we're done saving the kemana and all."

I wonder...

"Do you think I'm darker than the other day?" she asked.

"No, not that. Why do you ask?"

"I've had some breakthroughs with some of my Drow magic while I've been here," she explained. "Particularly with my shadow compression and healing. I wondered if it might have made a difference. If anything, I wonder if obsessing over Drae helped in a weird, roundabout way. It might have kept me thinking more like a Drow. I can't say it was the key to victory, but it definitely helped, and I'm not so sure I would have survived the explosion without using shadow healing."

"Any improvement's always useful, even if it is a little painful to earn it." The elf snickered. "At least we had a few days to relax before everything went all Brownstone and Berens on us. I actually considered last night whose luck to blame before I settled on it being a combination."

"I'm surprised anyone bothered to show up to work today," Alison admitted and glanced at the bartender. "The only reason I didn't leave right away is because I assumed the PDA and the FBI would want to chat and my room wasn't actually damaged. The staff said no one has to leave if they don't want to, and I've seen most of the employees during the last few days. Talk about dedication to service."

"Are you thinking about staying longer?" Izzie asked.

"I don't think that's a good idea, and it's hard to completely relax given everything that happened. Not only that, I think I need to lie low for a while. Even though it was all fake, I don't want too many people talking about my naked flying." She rolled her eyes.

Her friend snickered. "We'll leave soon. Luke's talked to the authorities. The staff all live in the area and very few of them fled when they had the chance. It makes sense. This is their home and they didn't want to leave to begin with."

"Their home, huh?" Alison sighed. "Is this the end? This place was already suffering. Will the repairs and cancelations be the end for them?"

"I can't say, but they're already talking about getting FEMA disaster money, and there are many experienced magicals, so they can repair numerous things even without money." Izzie smiled. "And Luke's talking to everyone in the government he possibly can to help them." She gestured in the general direction in the garden. "Because of how Jade did things, most of the damage was contained to the grounds. If she'd set off the explosion in town or the resort itself, things might be different. The staff seems hopeful, and Luke's already pledged publicly to come back. He gave a big political-style speech about how good people will never give in to terrorism and all that." She laughed. "If there's one thing he's good at, it's giving big speeches. From what he said, he thinks it might actually cause an uptick in people coming here because now, they'll know it'll be even safer than before because of what happened, but at the same time, they can pretend they're doing something dangerous. I don't see the appeal, but my life has been dangerous in the extreme so I'm a little jaded."

"Wait. Pledged publicly to come back?" She didn't like that sound of that. There were possibly serious implications.

The Jasper Elf nodded. "Yes. What about it?"

"What does that mean? Did he put something up on the Net?"

"Sure." Izzie shrugged. "But he mentioned it to the staff and the reporters as well."

Alison grimaced. "There are reporters here? Damn. I should have known. No wonder most guests left so quickly. Many of those types of people don't want reporters to harass them."

"Of course reporters came. It's not every day something happens like this, even to you. And of course, anything Alison Brownstone is involved in is big news. It doesn't help that a Berens is involved, too. Just because my parents aren't as flashy as your dad doesn't mean they're not famous. After all those years of hiding and not having to worry about that kind of thing, I now have to deal with the annoyances of fame exactly like you."

"Serves you right."

"It's enough to make me run off and start a bakery."

Alison raised an eyebrow. "A bakery?"

"What? You'd prefer a barbecue restaurant?"

"I simply didn't know you were that into baking."

"I'm not. It's only an example." Izzie laughed. "I should hang out with Yumfuck and have him do interviews. If I have to deal with the media, at least it'd be fun."

"A troll interview would be interesting. Weird, but interesting. I don't think most people who watch all those troll comedies understand how many of them there really are."

"It's funny how life works out." A wistful look settled over the elf's face. "My normal life was being the daughter of the Fixer, part Jasper Elf, and hanging out with a foul-mouthed troll. Then, my normal life was hiding from dark wizards for years. Now, I'm dating a shifter congressman and helping defeat giant eight-legged horses."

"Normal, huh?" Alison stared at her glass. "I don't know if I believe in that idea anymore. Fighting giant eight-legged horses might be my normal, but it's not like I want that to be my normal." She shook her head. "I'll give Jade a little credit—but only a little. She was right. She was better than New Veil since she didn't go for maximum carnage."

"That's a damned low bar."

"Isn't it, though?" She surveyed the empty bar. "I keep trying to remind myself that it's not every day that something like this happens."

"Not every day but every week?"

"Sure. I can't get greedy." She yawned. "It's been a long time since I pushed my magic so much. I feel like I could sleep for a week and still be tired."

"Only a week?" Izzie laughed. "I feel like I could sleep for a month. I don't think I could have pulled that off if we weren't in a kemana, even with all the Berens line power. That goes to show you these places aren't totally useless."

"Maybe, but that same higher background magical power is also why Jade could do what she did, even with the help of all her artifacts and technomagic gadgets. It's probably one of the reasons she spent so long choosing a target. It would have fizzled too quickly if she, say, targeted my building."

Her friend's smile vanished and she nodded. "From what I've heard, there were injuries here and there, but only two deaths—the security chief and one of the cops."

"That's what Mason told me, too." Alison shook her

head. "Even in my most paranoid dreams, I would never have thought one of Carlyle's people would have been involved in all this. It makes me think about all my enemies, everyone I've faced in the past, and when they'll come back. How can I be sure they're truly defeated? I've tried to move on by convincing myself I've gutted enough of certain groups that they'll never be a threat. That's the only way I can live because I can't watch my back all the time."

Izzie drained half her glass in one gulp. "No, you can't. I could barely do it with only one major enemy."

"That's cheery."

"That's simply the truth, Alison." She set her glass down. "But I know, for me, that I'm done living that way. I'll annihilate anyone stupid enough to attack me, but I absolutely will not sit there and constantly look over my shoulder for dark wizards. Alison, we're both strong but even we have our limits. You can't control the world, so why try? Sometimes, it's better to accept that both good and bad shit will happen."

"You're right." She sighed. "I keep thinking about my dad and how he's done a decent job of keeping things calm, but my mom has almost no issues. So there's proof right there that there doesn't have to be trouble. And now you tell me that. Mason's told me that for a while, if only because I always use it as an excuse to slow things down in our relationship."

"He's a good guy," her friend observed. "I was worried for the longest time about how things might turn out for you after what happened at school, but it's good to see you've finally moved on and you're even getting married. Assuming you don't keep stalling."

Alison swallowed. "I've been thinking about my wedding, especially this morning."

"Oh? Killing that monster has given you some ideas about your wedding? What, will you have an eight-legged horse cake?"

She shook her head. "Not exactly. It's only..." She frowned a little as she tried to find the right words. "The more I've thought about it, the less I'm interested in a big, spectacular wedding."

"And Mason is okay with that?"

"He says he doesn't care as long as I'm happy. But what about you? You won't be insulted if I don't have some huge wedding spectacular, right?"

Izzie offered her an incredulous look. "I'm the last person you need to worry about. You do what you need to, Alison. You've earned it. You can do something for yourself, you know. You don't have to think about everyone, especially for your wedding. Go be a Brownstone Bridezilla if you need to."

"For myself, huh?" The words lingered in her mind as she finished her wine.

CHAPTER TWENTY-FOUR

I t was good to be back home, but it was hard to relax when she read the news. Alison sighed where she lay on her side on her couch. Half the stories were directly or indirectly about the New Hampshire incident and the implications. The culprit being an AMS employee also resulted in a huge number of retrospective stories on Scott Carlyle and Alison's involvement, both in his experiment and stopping him. That, in turn, meant that every reporter in the country was interested in talking to her. Ava handled the media for her, and Tahir's help had made her phone manageable, but it was only so long that she could hide from the hungry news wolves.

Mason's right. I need to have a solid couple of weeks off-grid —no phone, no news, no worries, and no freaking giant monsters.

A high-pitched whine was accompanied by a pulse of magic and she knew immediately that someone had tripped one of her early warning wards. They didn't acti-vate simply because someone walked into the area. She didn't want that to happen every time a neighbor arrived.

The fact that the ward activated indicated someone not attuned to the ward had used magic.

She bounded to her feet, layered a shield, and held her arm out. Magic flowed to her hand and shadows coalesced into a dark blade.

You have to be kidding me! Even at home? Whoever it is, they'd better be normal size and have only two legs.

Mason stomped down the stairs, his wand in hand and his expression grim. "Please tell me it's Sonya messing around."

"I doubt it. When she called, she said wouldn't be back for a couple of hours and she knows better than to trip the wards." She listened for any sign of attack. For now, there'd been no explosions, no shouts, and no gunfire. That could either be a good start or the respite before a twenty-four-legged stone dragon barreled into her house and swallowed her whole.

Is every Brownstone required to have at least one house blown up?

Alison tossed her phone on the couch and her jaw tightened.

He frowned. "Shouldn't you call for reinforcements?"

"Whatever's happening will be over by the time anyone can come." She tilted her head when she felt a familiar sensation with a familiar texture. "Do you feel that?"

Could it be?

"It's definitely magic." He turned slowly and pointed his wand at the door. "I'm very sure it came from over there."

She crept toward the door, her blade ready. A light knock gave her pause and she scowled and looked at Mason.

"I expect more of a kick the door in or an explode inward type situation," she admitted.

He shrugged and held his wand at the ready. "Maybe they're polite assassins or they want to flip the house after they've killed you."

"Good luck in this real estate market." Alison approached the door cautiously, yanked it open, and jumped back, poised for an attack.

A beautiful dark-skinned woman with white hair and pointed ears stood on the other side. The Drow's loose white gown rippled in the slight summer wind. A bland smile adorned her face.

Her dark-eyed gaze settled on Alison's blade. "That's an aggressive greeting, Princess of the Shadow Forged. I won't claim deep knowledge of the culture of Earth kingdoms and its countries, but I do suspect that most encourage slightly better manners." Her attention shifted to Mason, haughty dismissal in her eyes. "You can do better. Just because you're half-human doesn't mean you need to be with one."

Alison stepped back and rolled her eyes. She released her blade and shield before she folded her arms. Honestly, she would have preferred a stone dragon. "Drae, I presume?"

The woman nodded once. "Yes, Drae, Princess of the Deepest Night. It's interesting to finally meet you, Princess of the Shadow Forged. Thus far, I find you're meeting my...uh, expectations."

She gestured to a chair. "You might as well come inside. Unless you're here to fight, of course. If that's the case, we can do it outside. I don't care if you can use magic to repair things. There's always something not quite the same. I can tell."

Mason lowered his wand and muttered under his breath.

Drae scoffed. "I'm not as barbaric as some of the other princesses you have encountered. Don't deal with me the way you'd deal with Rasila or Miar." She stepped inside, her movements graceful, and stared at Mason. "Will the human be here the entire time?"

"Learn to read the room." She glared at her. "He's my fiancé, you know, and his name is Mason, not 'the human.'"

"Yes, I have heard that you intend to marry a human." The visitor sighed. "That's your choice, as disappointing as it is, but it doesn't excuse his presence now. We're about to discuss Drow business, not human business, and royal business at that. I want him out of the room."

"It's okay, A," Mason stated coldly, his nose wrinkled in distaste. "I don't need to be here for this." He headed up the stairs. "And I don't want to be here for this."

The Drow waited until the bedroom door slammed. "That's much better. I know you'll tell him everything we're about to talk about anyway, but that doesn't mean I have to pretend to tolerate his presence." Her mouth curled into a frown. "Humans."

"You hate humans?" Alison asked.

"I find them arrogant and presumptuous considering how pathetic a species they are." Drae sat in the chair, crossed her legs, and rested her hands in her lap. "But that's irrelevant because I only intend to stay on Earth long enough to finish this discussion. The opening of the gates doesn't mean we need to demean ourselves with this backward planet. Of course, it's impossible to escape humans totally, even on Oriceran, but it's far easier since they don't infest the entire planet like they do here."

"You're a real bitch. Has anyone ever told you that?" She smiled as she said it. "Like top-level bitchery."

"A harsh truth remains a truth, no matter how you wish to label it." The woman simply tilted her head with a faint smile on her lips. The relaxed socialite look didn't do much to conceal the contempt that radiated from her eyes. "Given your contact with some of the other princesses, I decided it was time to put in an appearance—especially since everyone will make their moves soon enough. The better we understand each other, the more we can come to some mutually beneficial agreement."

"From the way I hear it, you don't even like me involved in the succession."

"I don't. You're not a Drow. You're something that merely happens to have Drow magic." Drae's tone dripped with disdain. "I don't care that your adopted father defeated Laena. She had led our people down a self-destructive path. In that sense, he did us a favor, but don't think that means I want your human-tainted hand involved in selecting the Drow queen. If by some corrupt mistake you were to become the queen, it would be the death of our people."

Alison sat on the arm of the couch, her arms folded. "You have a real way with people, you know. A painful way, but a way. I recently had to deal with a woman who summoned an army of monsters against innocent people, and I think I wanted to kill her less than I want to kill you."

"I'm not here to earn your approval or friendship,

Alison. If that's not clear, let me be explicit on that point."
The Drow raised her chin and scoffed.

She allowed herself a sneer in response. "Oh, I think you've done an excellent job of making that clear. You don't like me. Fine. Message received, Princess." She saluted. "My tainted half-breed ears can hear perfectly."

"If only it were so easy." Drae looked around the living room. "Seeing your home only confirms where your loyalties lie. Unfortunately, I've found that one should question the truths told them by outsiders—even those they trust—so I had to come here to make sure what I believed to be the truth was in fact that. This is merely another disappointment in a long line."

"It must be horrible to be you and have the entire world not bend to your expectations."

"On some days, yes." The visitor's expression somehow turned even more dismissive. "I have not come here to seek your support for the throne, nor would I want it even if you offered it. I don't need the support of a half-human. I will note, however, that if you're willing to renounce your title and submit to a ritual of a power transfer, I'll consider leaving you alone."

"Ritual of power transfer?" She narrowed her eyes.

"Yes. You will no longer be the Princess of the Shadow Forged. This isn't a mere political matter and it has magical implications."

"Why— Oh. I see. You're worried the next wish will go to a future daughter of mine, and she'll be even more human than me."

"Your line doesn't deserve the wish." Drae's nostrils

flared. "You wasted yours and your child would waste hers on frivolities as well. Do you know why?"

"Because we're not royal bitches whose names begin with D?"

The sophisticated beauty of the woman's features settled into harsh lines. "It's because you don't think like a Drow. The wish doesn't need to stay with your line, but as long as you continue as the Princess of the Shadow Forged, the future of the wish's dispensation will remain in doubt. But if you're obsessed with being human, you can commit to your human identity fully. In that case, a Drow princess would have no business with you."

"Being the Princess of the Shadow Forged is part of my mother's legacy," she replied and her hand shook slightly. She took a few breaths to calm her pounding heart. "As was the wish and any future wishes."

"Your mother—" Drae began.

Alison narrowed her eyes. "What about my mother? Choose your next words carefully, Drae, or you'll see exactly how human I can be."

"Forget her for now. Are you saying you refuse my generous offer?" The visitor shook her head. "I know you claim constant neutrality in the matter of the queen, but the only way you can truly not be involved is by following my suggestion. Otherwise, you will eventually be forced into the battle. Will you take up arms against Miar if she decides to support the Guardians? What if Rasila decides to fight her? Drow are passionate, not spineless and weak like humans. If a true struggle comes, there will be bloodshed and not only royal blood. If you wish to avoid it, Alison, take my offer."

She managed to unclench her jaw, but her next sentence came out in a low and sinister tone. "I'll tell you what I've told the others. I'm neutral and I intend to stay that way." She narrowed her eyes. "But that doesn't mean I'll give my title up or let any of you push me around."

"Your title means nothing on Earth. There are only a handful of Drow here. The wish isn't meant for use on Earth. It's meant to aid the Drow."

"It means everything," Alison replied. "As for the wish, my mother died protecting that legacy because she didn't want it to be misused. She died even though she could have used it to save her life."

Disapproval flashed across Drae's face. "That's it, then. You refuse?"

"I do. You'll simply have to accept that. If you think you can force me to accept it, keep in mind that I'm fairly upset at the moment about not having a nice vacation."

The Drow sighed. "I suspected as such. You're stubborn. And, no, I won't insult you with simple threats. Whatever I feel about your true nature, I can't deny your power. The most recent situation you referenced is merely one of many that confirm it."

Her visitor arched an eyebrow, the smug half-smile worthy of a punch. But something about the woman's confidence fueled old paranoia.

"And you had nothing to do with that?" she asked. "It doesn't seem likely that a Drow princess who hates humans would work with a human who is suspicious of magicals, but like they say on Earth, 'The enemy of my enemy is my friend.'"

Drae snorted. "There's some mild wisdom lingering

among the inferior, after all. I'll be straightforward with you because it costs me nothing at this time. I had considered attempting something at the resort—nothing serious, merely a challenge to your abilities. As much as I disdain Earth, I do have agents with knowledge of its ways, and a kemana resort presented an excellent target. But, no, I didn't implement my plan. Apparently, that was wise, as you were tested anyway and I didn't have to expend any resources. I couldn't risk angering the American government. I can't risk that...yet, at least."

"I won't even bother to ask for a truth spell. You're such a smug bitch, I don't think you've even bothered to lie to me right now, but I'm still surprised you would admit to something like that."

"I've studied you. You won't attack me for stating the truth. I understand how your mind works, Alison."

"Do you now?" She tapped the side of her head. "It gets fairly complicated in here. You might be surprised."

"I've harmed no one you care about. I've hurt no innocent humans." Drae's expression turned dour. "What would you have to gain by attacking me? Right now, my actions don't affect you or this pathetic planet. I don't desire you as an enemy, but your demonstrated lack of care about the succession does make me wonder how truly committed you are to your path of neutrality." She studied her with a hungry look. "I have an alternative suggestion."

"Is this where we become allies? Because I don't like you and I won't help you become queen."

"No. Everything I said stands, but I understand your desire to honor your mother and why that might make you keep your status and title. I suggest a compromise." Drae unfolded her hands and held her palm out. A dark circle appeared and partially disappeared. "My primary concern is not having you interfere with the succession. We could use a mutual binding ritual in which neither of us will be able to target the other for six months. You would pledge, also through magic, to not involve yourself in the succession under any circumstances, and I can also pledge to not target you but also others of importance to you."

"Six months?" she asked.

Drae nodded. "I won't strip you of anything permanently, and neither of us will agree to become perpetual allies."

Alison shook her head. "No deal."

Her visitor snorted. "You're so intransigent, or perhaps you care more about being the future queen than you claim. Why delay the inevitable? Tell me who you support—Miar or Rasila? Or perhaps the Guardians?"

"I am what I've said, neutral for now. I consider Miar and Rasila friends. I don't know enough about the current Guardians' policies to support them, but I learned something when I was younger about the Drow."

"And what is that?" the woman asked.

"If a Brownstone ignores Drow stuff, it comes back to bite them in the ass."

"Ah," her visitor murmured. "You speak of Laena's machinations and attacks."

"Among other things." She shrugged.

"Novati would see Laena restored. Did you know that?"

"Yeah. I've heard it mentioned as a possibility."

Drae gestured toward the stairs. "If Laena is restored, the Drow would attack the Brownstones and all your allies in force. Her honor would demand it. No matter how powerful you are individually, you cannot win against an entire race."

She gritted her teeth. "Then Novati should stay the hell out of my way."

"Yes, she should." The Drow stood and her half-smile returned. "I think you need more time to consider the implications. I'll return in the future. I think this was a good conversation, and we now both understand each other better."

Alison pushed off the couch and headed toward her front door. "So what does this mean between us? You already admitted you're plotting against me."

"Not in the sense you should worry about. As yet, you haven't done anything to warrant my extreme attention."

She opened the front door. "Is that a threat?"

"Simply a statement of fact."

Drae stepped outside and walked several yards away. She raised her arm and murmured quietly under her breath. A portal shuddered open.

"Peace isn't always about avoiding battle, Princess of the Shadow Forged," she declared and slipped through the gateway.

"Don't I know it." She sighed as it closed.

CHAPTER TWENTY-FIVE

This is ridiculous. Rasila's screwing with me now. I can't believe she dragged us here of all places.

The other Drow princess clutched her putter, her eyes narrowed and her face a mask of concentration. Mini-golf was war, and it was time for her first hole-in-one. She held her breath as the blades of a fake windmill turned to expose and block the hole in an alternating pattern.

Three Drow princesses playing mini-golf would be a bizarre sight, but Rasila and Miar both wore their human visages and their natural shapeshifting provided perfect disguises. Ironically, they stood out less than Alison with her undyeable white hair.

Rasila hit the ball. It cruised over the green toward the windmill. The blade passed in front of the hole, but it moved as the ball arrived. It continued, passed through the narrow aperture, and dropped into the hole.

"I thought you said this game was good martial training," Miar grumbled. "I don't understand how this improves battle skills."

"It teaches precision," Rasila insisted. "And patience. It also forces one to make critical decisions."

"I find that dubious." The other princess teed up. She smacked her ball and it careened into the windmill and bounced back, which drew a hiss of irritation. Rasila snickered.

"We need to talk about the actual reason I called you." Alison looked around. No one else was on the course, and her companions had cast silence spells at each of the first few holes, using magic to keep their conversation private but then didn't actually seem to want to discuss sensitive Drow matters. At this point, she was convinced Rasila only wanted to have a princesses' day out at the course.

"A six-month binding ritual," Rasila murmured and shook her head. "Things are moving into the final stage. All our positioning will soon become useful. Whatever Drae's planning will be long over by then, which suggests she's far more ready than we've realized."

Miar grunted as she chipped her ball into the hole. "It could be a trick. She might have made the offer knowing Alison would refuse and also knowing she would pass the information onto us to sow panic. If we're nervous, we might take hasty action and she can exploit that."

"That's a possibility," Rasila commented. "She does love a good manipulation."

Alison rolled her eyes. "What about you?"

The Drow grinned. "I love an excellent manipulation, but I'm far more pleasant than her."

"When you're not trying to kill people, sure."

Miar retrieved her ball and walked to the next hole. She

took a moment to cast a privacy spell before she spoke. "We also can't ignore the possibility that she's telling the truth. If she is, it means we're running out of time and we need to strongly consider our relationships and alliances." She looked at Alison. "I understand you don't want to be queen, but you should throw your support formally behind one of the other candidates or at least formally support the Guardians."

Rasila studied Miar. "And what would you do if she supported the Guardians?"

The other Drow squared her shoulders. "I might consider giving them my formal support as well."

"The Drow ruled by a council? What madness."

"Would you prefer the rule of Drae or Laena? Novati is already gathering Laena supporters." Miar set her ball down. The latest obstacle was a purple squid whose tentacles rose and fell at random. She tapped her ball, and it rolled through the tentacle forest and slowed to a stop inches from the hole. While she didn't quite grin, she did grunt in approval.

"I'm not ready to make any decisions," Alison explained. "Not until I have a better idea of what Drae might do and even what the Drow people want."

Rasila sneered. "The Drow aren't supporters of your American democracy, Alison. What they want is to be led by a strong woman. It is our job as princesses to ensure the best woman becomes queen, not to worry about our subjects' feelings. Please note your potential benefits in this."

"Such as?"

The woman paused her response while she took her putt. Her ball bounced off an errant tentacle and she frowned. "If I or Miar become queen, you and your allies are at least nominally safe. Arguably, the same is true of the Guardians. They only gained power because of the actions of your father. Attacking your family would implicitly signal that Laena's removal was illegitimate. Drae has made it clear she despises you and has only not attacked you out of temporary strategic considerations. Even if Novati doesn't restore Laena, she bears you ill will. Total neutrality increases the chance that Novati, Laena, or Drae will become queen and that increases your personal risk and that of your family and allies."

Alison sighed. "I understand that, but I still need time to think this all through. Whatever I choose will alter the course of Drow history for centuries."

"Don't take too long," Miar advised. She nodded at Alison's putter. "Either for your turn or your decision. Drae or Novati might not kill another princess, but they have no problem exiling them or killing their supporters and loved ones. If they win the succession struggle, there might be little we can do to aid you, and if Laena is restored, terror will come to Earth."

"Do you know what I need?" she asked as she struck her ball. It bounced off a back wall and fell into the hole.

Rasila frowned at it. "What?"

"An actual real vacation. It'd give me some time to think. It's kind of hard to make decisions when people are screwing with you and you have to fight armies of monsters."

The other princess chuckled but Miar scoffed. "This is no time to relax, Alison. It's time for careful planning and preparation."

She smiled. "I actually think it's more time for a nice hammock."

CHAPTER TWENTY-SIX

Not a single cloud dared to mar Alison's blue sky. The sun shone brightly, but the ocean breeze blew off the ocean toward the cabana and refreshed the air. Alison's head lay on her hands as she curled in the hammock hung between two palm trees, her mind a pleasant blank thanks to no distractions and a few margaritas.

Mason strolled up the beach in only his trunks. Sunlight glinted off water droplets and highlighted his firm muscles. It wasn't like she loved him only for his body, but it didn't hurt that he was like a Greek statue come to life.

He grinned as he neared her. "You still look ridiculous in that getup, A."

She adjusted her long black wig and the oversized sunglasses that covered half her face. "They keep me out of sight, right? All it takes is one drone to see me, and the next thing, we'll have paparazzi drones flocking the area to try to get pictures. This way, at least I haven't used any spells that might attract attention. I can sit here and enjoy our actual vacation. I'm finally relaxed, exactly like you wanted me to be."

"We've managed to make it a week without naked Drow, fake murders, or major battles. I think we'll actually succeed this time, even if I have to resist laughing every time I see your disguise."

"You're right." She sat and slid out of the hammock, stretched, and enjoyed his lingering gaze on her toned body in her black bikini. "Nothing exotic. No giant monsters, no super-technomagic armor, no gangsters, no Drow assassins, no missing friends kidnapped in foreign countries, and no dark wizards."

"I don't know about the last one." He grimaced. "That shrimp last night was so bad, a curse had to be involved."

Alison laughed. "The tuna was great. It's weird. My dad goes on and on and on about KISS, but this is one time I can see the attraction. I haven't been this relaxed in a long time. Now it might turn out that the Brownstone building was blown up yesterday and Ava merely didn't want to interrupt me, but at least for now, I don't even have to pretend to care. That's the real fun in this."

"Keep it simple," Mason murmured. He chuckled and shook his head. "For a guy who likes to keep things simple, his wedding was ridiculous."

"That's technically Mom's fault. He was responsible for the proposal but remember, she was the one mostly responsible for almost everything not priest—or barbecue —related at the wedding." She smiled. "Speaking of simple, I have a crazy idea."

"As long as it doesn't involve attacking giant eight-legged stone horses, I'm all in."

She walked over to him and rested her head against his chest, enjoying the soothing thump of his heart. "I'm not my dad, but I'm also not my mom."

He kissed the top of her head and placed an arm around her. "I've noticed. They cuss far more than you do and threaten to kill people more often."

"I simply want to get married," she whispered. "I don't want to do anything special. I've already checked with my parents, and they don't care. You told me before you didn't care, but are you sure? What about your parents?"

"My parents will care, but they'll get over it," he replied. "What are you thinking?"

"A quick trip to Vegas. If you're fine with it, that is. Oh, and I did some thinking about something else we haven't really nailed down." She sighed and looked up. "I want to keep the Brownstone name. It's…I don't know. It's weird to articulate it all. I owe him too much to give his name up."

Mason laughed. "It's fine. I'm marrying you because I want to stay with you for the rest of my life, not because I want everyone to call you Mrs Lind." He cupped her face with his hands and gave her a deep kiss. "I've wanted this for a while, Alison, and if I can get it quicker by going to Vegas and you keeping the Brownstone name, that's a cheap price as far as I'm concerned. Are you sure you don't want to simply go back to Seattle and visit the courthouse?"

Alison shook her head firmly. "No, I like the idea of a crazy Vegas wedding. Everyone's so convinced I can't be spontaneous."

He smirked and looked away.

"What?" She frowned.

"A, it doesn't count as spontaneous if you spend months thinking about it before you decide on it."

She rolled her eyes. "Whatever. We have another whole week scheduled for the vacation. I say we book a flight and a hotel tomorrow and we tie the knot. I don't want to tell anyone until we're finished with this little vacation. It'll be a big surprise that way."

"Only a week's honeymoon?"

"We'll play it by ear." She shrugged and grinned. "How's that for spontaneous?"

"I like anything that ends with me spending more time alone with you."

Alison smiled as Mason opened the door for her and gestured for her to enter.

"After you," he suggested. "I'm still kind of iffy on this, but it's your call."

She stepped inside and drew a few curious stares from the patrons of the small barbecue restaurant. After all, most people didn't eat barbecue in a white wedding dress. They gave her a startled once-over before they returned to their ribs, brisket, and pulled pork. While most people didn't eat barbecue in their wedding regalia, they were in Las Vegas. Countless far more unusual characters had eaten at the place in the decades it had been open.

"Jesse Rae's is kind of a Brownstone wedding tradition," she insisted, headed to the front counter, and smiled at the employee. "Good evening."

The woman smiled in response. "It's been a while,

Alison. I wish Mike were here, but I'll have to take a picture of you in that dress." She laughed. "He'll probably be happy you showed up even if he didn't get to cater your wedding."

She waved a hand. "Don't worry. It was a quickie kind of thing. No one catered it. But you can surprise us with the food. I'm trying to be spontaneous this week."

Mason pulled a chair out.

Alison sat quickly. "Thanks, dear." She snickered.

He made a face. "No. I don't think that'll work unless I can start calling you 'wife' all the time. Hey, wife, where are my slippers?" He laughed.

She removed her veil and placed it on a nearby chair. "I thought about sushi, but if I keep the name, I might as well keep the tradition."

"How does it feel?" he asked.

"I don't know. Good, but not different?" She looked at her wedding ring. "It was mighty convenient of you to have the ring ready. Did you plan on some spontaneous marriage ceremony yourself during the trip?"

In response, he whistled innocently. "Hey, a good husband's always prepared. After that resort debacle, I couldn't be sure when we'd have a good opportunity, but you know how I am. I didn't want to pressure you. The real question is our honeymoon. I thought you'd want some-where a little more relaxed than Vegas. It's only a matter of time before someone realizes Alison Brownstone's in town and she got married."

"You're right." She finally tore her eyes away from the wedding ring. "Plus, I can't get married and not visit Trey, Zoe, and the others, and Dad and Mom will want us to at least put in an appearance, not to mention your parents. I say we make a few quick visits during the next few days and take a good month for a honeymoon."

"A month?" He leaned forward and stared at her with an expression of dramatic astonishment. "Are you actually Alison, or are you Drae in disguise?"

"Very funny, dear."

Mason shuddered. "Don't do that. It's creepy, wife."

"Whatever you say, dear." She smirked. "I called Ava earlier. Nothing will collapse if we're gone for a month. She even has reservations set up for us. It's back to the island, hammock, and cabana with no phones and no pressure, only a newlywed couple with considerable time to fill."

"I like the sound of that. I really like the sound of that." A grin split his face. "And if a one-hundred-foot shark attacks the island?"

"Then we'll kill it, chop it up, and grill it." She nodded firmly, liking the plan. "Nothing short of a worldwide invasion will mess up our honeymoon."

"And if there is an invasion?" he asked.

"I'll give them a week to do their thing before we get out of bed."

The story is far from over. Alison and Mason may have gotten married, but that doesn't mean their adventures end there. Far from it. There's still the matter of the Drow succession to be sorted out and a dangerous trip to Mongolia to help out an old friend. Follow the adventures in DROW CONQUERER!

Get sneak peeks, exclusive giveaways, behind the scenes content, and more.
PLUS you'll be notified of special **one day only fan pricing** on new releases.

Sign up today to get free stories.

CLICK HERE

or visit: https://marthacarr.com/read-free-stories/

For Hire: Teachers for special school in Virginia countryside.

Must be able to handle teenagers with special abilities.

Cannot be afraid to discipline werewolves, wizards, elves and other assorted hormonal teens.

Apply at the School of Necessary Magic.

It's been one year since I moved into the dream house and a lot has happened. I retired from the day job, got another dog – the sweet pittie - Leela, the Offspring got engaged to the wonderful Jackie, I did far more traveling than I expected, my oldest sister, Diana died suddenly (that one event marked the year with more growth than anything else) – and *a lot* of books were published.

Those are just the highlights, and all they give you is a list of events.

What I really learned was to once again appreciate where I am and make sure I go out and live a life with actual humans – as well as revel in the wonderful Reader community that keeps evolving. In other words, balance in everything.

As a result, there were four other women here last night watching the finale of Bachelors in Paradise. JPJ does some serious man tears when he's not challenging someone to some strong chest bumping. Just saying. It was a show I had never seen before I made a point of getting to know my neighbors. Now, I have a new crew of friends who live really close by.

Tomorrow night I'm going on a first date – insert stomach in throat – and my goal is to just be myself. Full on Nerdette with charm (my vision of myself) who's very curious about everything and generally very optimistic. I figure that's an achievable goal for the night and anything else is a bonus. I'll let you know later if I pull it off. (I am cheating a little with a blowout for my hair – the women reading this will know what I'm talking about – and I figure, hey, if it lasts he can find out later that my hair is actually kind of curly.)

Last weekend there was another crew of authors hanging out in the house for the weekend sharing new ideas and using the hive mind to hunt for solutions. It was nice to see the dream house being put to good use. It's the point, for me, of having this big place. Open the doors and let in the people – and the dogs love it!

I'm also still out here running. Determined to get to a place where I can run a 5k without stopping. It's been a stop and start effort so far, but I'm signed up for the Hot Chocolate in Chicago in November along with a few friends. Here's hoping that helps me get to the finish line…

Really, all of life is a long journey that twists and turns and overall, mine is a great one. I know that some of that has to do with how I look at the world – and a lot of it has to do with the people who surround me. Great neighbors, the Offspring, great people like Michael Anderle to work with, and great Fans like all of you.

Okay, I have to run – off to look for a dress for tomorrow night. Wish me luck. More adventures to follow.

Thank you for reading Alison Brownstone THIS FAR into the series

I hope it says more about the stories, than your ability to sludge through to the finish line... But I'm ok with your abilities if that is part of the charm you have ;-)

It's Sunday afternoon and I'm up in The Cave in the Sky™ here in Las Vegas. I'm listening to songs by a new band (for me) called Danheim that C.M. Simpson turned me on to. Part of the reason the songs work for us (authors) is that we CAN'T understand the lyrics (they are in Icelandic I'm told... Sounds really cool and historic to me.)

If we can understand the lyrics, then sometimes they take us out of our writing zone and that's a no-no.

I like the driving beats, drums and push. They are a part Neolithic I feel and part David Arkenstone. All in all?

Cool stuff.

I was finishing the beats for Witch of the Federation

Book 04. Story 02 (or 04.02) yesterday and needed 18 chapters of ideas.

I had just gone out to lunch with Jonathan Brazee to talk about life and our next series after the Bohica Chronicles (ZOO Universe) and needed a nap.

Too much Chinese food – very similar to too much Turkey at Thanksgiving.

It was nap time. I could work on the beats AFTER my nap. Plus, I had no major ideas of exactly where to take the rest of the story. Collen (C.M.) mentioned she was listening to the music for her present work in process and I thought, 'why not'? I went to Apple Music and bought their latest album to support their efforts on YouTube (giving their music away.)

Then, turned and told Alexa to "Play music by Danheim".

Seconds later, I laid down on the office couch for 'just a moment of shut-eye.' That was a laugh, I think it was about an hour and a half of shuteye.

Danheim was playing the whole time.

Once I got up, kissed my wife hello and went back to my office and got in front of the laptop, I busted out almost forty scenes of work in about four hours...

Mission accomplished.

Today I'm reviewing ads, ad spending, publishing calendar, video work for 'Advertising City' and I'm writing author notes while emailing a company in Austin to possibly use their IP for a set of stories in 2020.

I've had calls with Martha, Craig Martelle, David Beers, and about to speak to Jude (3D artist) in about 30 minutes.

Somewhere in this, I'm grabbing another nap!

In fact, I think I'll grab that nap right now… Danheim is playing and it is lulling me to sleep.

Ad Aeternitatem,

Michael Anderle

Series in the Oriceran Universe:

SCHOOL OF NECESSARY MAGIC
SCHOOL OF NECESSARY MAGIC: RAINE CAMPBELL
ALISON BROWNSTONE
THE DANIEL CODEX SERIES
THE LEIRA CHRONICLES
I FEAR NO EVIL
FEDERAL AGENTS OF MAGIC
THE UNBELIEVABLE MR. BROWNSTONE
REWRITING JUSTICE
THE KACY CHRONICLES
MIDWEST MAGIC CHRONICLES
SOUL STONE MAGE
THE FAIRHAVEN CHRONICLES

Other series:

THE LAST VAMPIRE

BOOKS BY MICHAEL ANDERLE

For a complete list of books by Michael Anderle, please visit

www.lmbpn.com/ma-books/

All LMBPN Audiobooks are Available at Audible.com and
iTunes. For a complete list of audiobooks visit:

www.lmbpn.com/audible